THIS IS WHAT SHE'D WANTED.
THIS IS WHAT SHE'D FEARED...

Quivers of longing leapt from one to the other as Tif slipped his hand beneath her shirt and deftly stroked the satiny skin of her midriff. His tentative quest sparked an urgency between them. Andra felt him tense from head to foot, then trembled as his mouth feverishly brushed her throat. It seemed as if her entire being was centered on contact with the heated stirring of his body. Within the shadows of the night, she was aware only of the length of his hard thigh thrust against hers, the warmth of his lips clinging to hers. Their sudden, restless intimacy dizzied her and sent her plunging into an overwhelming delirium.

A CANDLELIGHT ECSTASY ROMANCE ®

106 INTIMATE STRANGERS, *Denise Mathews*
107 BRAND OF PASSION, *Shirley Hart*
108 WILD ROSES, *Sheila Paulos*
109 WHERE THE RIVER BENDS, *Jo Calloway*
110 PASSION'S PRICE, *Donna Kimel Vitek*
111 STOLEN PROMISES, *Barbara Andrews*
112 SING TO ME OF LOVE, *JoAnna Brandon*
113 A LOVING ARRANGEMENT, *Diana Blayne*
114 LOVER FROM THE SEA, *Bonnie Drake*
115 IN THE ARMS OF LOVE, *Alexis Hill*
116 CAUGHT IN THE RAIN, *Shirley Hart*
117 WHEN NEXT WE LOVE, *Heather Graham*
118 TO HAVE AND TO HOLD, *Lori Herter*
119 HEART'S SHADOW, *Prudence Martin*
120 THAT CERTAIN SUMMER, *Emma Bennett*
121 DAWN'S PROMISE, *Jo Calloway*
122 A SILENT WONDER, *Samantha Hughes*
123 WILD RHAPSODY, *Shirley Hart*
124 AN AFFAIR TO REMEMBER, *Barbara Cameron*
125 TENDER TAMING, *Heather Graham*
126 LEGACY OF LOVE, *Tate McKenna*
127 THIS BITTERSWEET LOVE, *Barbara Andrews*
128 A GENTLE WHISPER, *Eleanor Woods*
129 LOVE ON ANY TERMS, *Nell Kincaid*
130 CONFLICT OF INTEREST, *Jayne Castle*
131 RUN BEFORE THE WIND, *Joellyn Carroll*
132 THE SILVER FOX, *Bonnie Drake*
133 WITH TIME AND TENDERNESS, *Tira Lacy*
134 PLAYING FOR KEEPS, *Lori Copeland*
135 BY PASSION BOUND, *Emma Bennett*
136 DANGEROUS EMBRACE, *Donna Kimel Vitek*
137 LOVE SONG, *Prudence Martin*
138 WHITE SAND, WILD SEA, *Diana Blayne*
139 RIVER ENCHANTMENT, *Emma Bennett*
140 PORTRAIT OF MY LOVE, *Emily Elliott*
141 LOVING EXILE, *Eleanor Woods*
142 KINDLE THE FIRES, *Tate McKenna*
143 PASSIONATE APPEAL, *Elise Randolph*
144 SURRENDER TO THE NIGHT, *Shirley Hart*
145 CACTUS ROSE, *Margaret Dobson*

MOONLIGHT RAPTURE

Prudence Martin

A CANDLELIGHT ECSTASY ROMANCE ®

This book could not have been written without the help of my more adventuresome friends. With thanks to Russell, Tyle, and Jan.

Published by
Dell Publishing Co., Inc.
1 Dag Hammarskjold Plaza
New York, New York 10017

Copyright © 1983 by Prudence Lichte

All rights reserved. No part of this book may be
reproduced or transmitted in any form or by any
means, electronic or mechanical, including photocopying,
recording, or by any information storage
and retrieval system, without the written permission
of the Publisher, except where permitted by law.

Dell ® TM 681510, Dell Publishing Co., Inc.
Candlelight Ecstasy Romance®, 1,203,540, is a registered
trademark of Dell Publishing Co., Inc.,
New York, New York.

ISBN: 0-440-15825-7

Printed in the United States of America
First printing—June 1983

To Our Readers:

We have been delighted with your enthusiastic response to Candlelight Ecstasy Romances®, and we thank you for the interest you have shown in this exciting series.

In the upcoming months we will continue to present the distinctive sensuous love stories you have come to expect only from Ecstasy. We look forward to bringing you many more books from your favorite authors and also the very finest work from new authors of contemporary romantic fiction.

As always, we are striving to present the unique, absorbing love stories that you enjoy most—books that are more than ordinary romance.

Your suggestions and comments are always welcome. Please write to us at the address below.

Sincerely,

The Editors
Candlelight Romances
1 Dag Hammarskjold Plaza
New York, New York 10017

CHAPTER ONE

This was where she'd come to find herself?

Andra looked from the broad, sloping launch site to the rest of Lee's Ferry, which consisted of little more than a trailer cafe-store, a ranger station, and a crowded campground. The clamor of massive silver-gray pontoon boats pushing off into the Colorado River covered the release of her heavy sigh. Why, she asked herself, had she ever listened to Rick?

Doubts about the wisdom of this vacation had been growing steadily over the past hour. She might as well attempt climbing Mount Everest, for all she knew about river rafting. A pair of well-browned, firmly muscled boatmen strolled past her, and her doubts solidified. What did she know about the wilderness, for Pete's sake? The most outdoorsy thing she'd ever done was walk the dog in Swope Park! Sleeping bags, packs, campfires, were as foreign to her as equipment for flying to the moon.

A heavyset man with what appeared to be an entire camera store strung around his neck pushed her rudely to the side and snapped several shots of the latest pontoon to hit the water. Mentally cursing Rick Paisley for deserting her, even momentarily, in this circuslike resort, Andra turned away and began to walk slowly toward the trailer cafe. Perhaps it would still be possible to back out. She'd tell Rick it had been a mistake—after all, hadn't she been adamant in her refusal when he'd first suggested it? That day, she remembered, she'd told him flat out that her sedentary soul wasn't suited to white-water rafting. It had been at least a decade since she'd even gone on a picnic. Just how had he convinced her to go rafting in the Grand Canyon?

The torrid noontime sun seemed to have selected her neck to bake; the short ends of her ash-brown hair stuck damply together. Andra raked her beautifully manicured and polished nails through her curls, recalling the sob story Rick had shed to persuade her to come. His current girl had eloped with some truck driver from Tennessee, leaving him with a paid trip for two down the Colorado River. For several weeks he'd been nagging Andy to go with him. Not that his repeated pleas had moved her. No, she reluctantly had to admit that she'd made the decision to go all by herself.

After years of being certain of herself, of what she wanted out of life, Andra had recently begun suffering self-doubts. She refused to believe it had anything to do with passing her thirtieth birthday. Unlike many of her friends, she was not frightened or repelled by the thought of aging. She knew she looked much younger than thirty—there were no wrinkles (if one discounted the crease which furrowed her brow in times of anger or reflection), no bulges in her slim figure. The only silver in her short, windswept hair was the natural ashen sheen she'd been born with. But despite all that, or perhaps because of it, for the first time in her life Andy had begun to question herself. She wondered whether her choices of law school and career—firmly decided upon while she was still a teenager—had been the right ones, after all.

Going through cases, meeting clients, Andra had given no outward hint of the vague restlessness growing within her. But her uncertainty increased until she knew she must do something to discover why such doubts were plaguing her. Returning to the firm one day after a particularly bad session in court, Andy grabbed her phone and buzzed Rick's adjoining office.

"Have you found someone to take on that raft trip yet?" she demanded as one asking if the execution's been completed.

"No," he replied with a surprised but ready laugh. "I must be losing my touch—it seems these days I can't even find anyone to take to a movie!"

"Good. I'm going," said Andra and hung up.

It was pure impulse, but later consideration didn't change her mind. By doing something totally out of her experience, she hoped to come to terms with herself, find out why she felt so unsettled with her life, with her career as an attorney. For two weeks she'd be away from family, friends, co-workers, clients, cases, everything which made her who and what she was. For two weeks she'd simply be Andra James. Whoever that might be.

Another bus pulled sluggishly into view and discharged a load of passengers, most looking as awkwardly lost as she. All her rationalizations for embarking on this trip now seemed as substantial as the puffs of dust hovering beneath the vehicle's wheels. Before she could execute her urge to throw herself in that bus and beg to be taken back to Kansas City, a hand gripped her arm and dragged her past the gawking strangers.

"Are you trying to get lost? We're forming over here. It's a good group so far, no real turkeys that I can tell," said Rick as he pulled her along. He bent his head toward her and grinned. "Except for you, that is."

Having been told by Rick that experienced boatmen refer to all first-time, obvious tourists as "turkeys," Andy knew she was being insulted. She didn't care. The only thing she cared about was leaving. Now, while she still had a chance.

"Rick, I don't think . . ." she gasped out, but he wasn't listening. He towed her with expert ease through the crowds, leaving her little choice but to move with him. She was amazed at how well he fit into the rugged atmosphere here. But then, she'd always thought he looked incongruous in the three-piece suits he wore in court, rather as if someone had stuffed his brawny frame into the well-tailored clothes by mistake. Rick was built like a wrestler, had the face of a friendly bulldog, and now looked perfectly natural in faded jeans, cotton blue shirt, and smudged canvas shoes.

He was busily running on about the size and makeup of their particular raft group, most of which failed to penetrate Andy's ever-increasing fear. Rick did, however, manage to convey that theirs would be a set of five oar-powered rafts. *Small,* rubber rafts. The large, motorized pontoons which had looked so frightening to her earlier suddenly assumed the glowing memory of a first love. Each raft, explained Rick, would hold four passengers and an oarsman, for a total group of twenty-five. He sounded gleeful. That anyone could be so energetically cheerful when the temperature was well over a hundred and the heated air resounded with babbling, shrieking, never-ending noise held Andra in an amazed silence.

He jerked her to a halt. Andra somewhat dazedly saw that she was in the midst of several youthful, blue-jeaned people, all of whom looked repulsively eager.

"This is Andra," Rick announced, "but don't worry. She's a lot tougher than she looks."

As everyone greeted her with a laugh, Andy smiled feebly and yearned to give Rick a swift kick. This would be, she promised herself, the last time she let him talk her into so much as going to lunch. Names flew at her and past her; she made no attempt to sort out who was who. She stood docilely, hearing but not listening as Rick chatted with the others, feeling a newfound empathy with the convicted.

"Here, put this on and keep it on," ordered Rick, thrusting a wad of orange canvas at her. "We're next to put in, so don't wander away."

"I'd like to know where I could wander to in this godforsaken place," she muttered, but she donned the life jacket and tied it securely about her midriff. "How long will it be?"

"The oarsmen are nearly finished packing in our gear. Once everything's lashed down, they'll lift the rafts into the water and we'll hop on and go."

Though he answered her, it was obvious Rick's attention was on the action of the crew as they clipped and lashed equipment on the inflated rafts. Andy saw a sparkling flash as the sun raced over a gold earring in the left ear of one oarsman and looked more closely at the men who would be responsible for her over the next two weeks. The man with the earring had long hair neatly tied at the nape with a leather thong just a shade darker than his sinewy back. Beside him, corded arms working with fluid ease, was a tall, thin man with a drooping mustache hanging above a cheery grin. Her eyes swept past two similarly hirsute specimens to pause on a pair of well-knit masculine thighs.

Long and bare, browned by the sun beyond the ragged edge of denim cutoffs, those legs mesmerized Andy. The smooth, powerful play of the muscles as they flexed, the occasional sun-glint of golden gossamer hair, the thin sheen of perspiration—all fascinated her. She let her eyes drift slowly upward, enjoying the simple beauty of a fine-toned body in action. She was not disappointed. The hips and waist were trim, and even the bulging lifejacket couldn't mask the shapely breadth of the bared back. All the strength she'd admired in the legs was fully displayed in the lithe motion of the solidly muscular arms. The thick column of his neck was hidden by layers of blond hair bleached to a startling near-white.

Turn, please turn. Let me look at you, thought Andra with an intensity which unnerved her.

As if he'd heard her unspoken plea, the man slowly straightened and quarter-turned, looking over his shoulder directly at her. Narrow, downturned eyes squinted at her from beneath straight pale brows. His long nose had an odd crook to it, as if it had been broken sometime, and ended with a small tilt above squared lips which were frowning slightly. The tousled blond hair appeared iridescent in contrast to the tawny plane of his clean-shaven cheeks.

It was not, however, due to any of these things that Andra gasped. Or rather, it was because of all of them. Within two seconds of peering across the short distance separating them, Andy had caught Rick's blue sleeve and turned, pulling him away from the crowd.

"What the hell," he began, clearly exasperated.

"I can't go," announced Andy, breaking off his protest with her frantic hiss.

"What do you mean? Of course you can. I've told you—"

"I don't mean I can't go rafting! I mean, I can't go with *him.*" She jerked her head in the general direction of the oarsmen.

"With who?" His tone was half-bewildered, half-irritated.

"Do you remember the Wilson divorce I handled? Just over two years ago?"

Rick's fine, sparse dark hair was rapidly receding beyond the point of no return, a condition he didn't improve by constantly yanking at it with one beefy hand. He did so now as he demanded, "What's that got to do with anything? Look, Andy, I haven't come all this way to indulge in some—"

"Rick! Will you listen? It's *him!* It's Theodore Wilson." Andy again tugged at his sleeve and pointed at the crew. "The one with the bleached blond hair. You must remember that case! It was the messiest divorce I ever took on—he fought it every step of the way, and his poor wife was practically neurotic by the time it was all over."

He cast one quick glance at the man, then focused a puzzled gaze on her. "So?"

"So!" she fairly screeched. "So this is the man who nearly tore my apartment to pieces. You've got to remember it, Rick. His wife had nowhere to go, and he was harassing her unmercifully, so I let her stay with me for a while. He came looking for her and forced his way in. He was drunk and wouldn't believe that she'd already moved into a place of her own. Oh, god, why did *he* have to be here?"

"Are you sure, Andy? If this is the same guy who ransacked your place, why did you agree to come on the trip?" Rick sounded as if she were at fault, and Andra responded with a look that would have sizzled bacon at forty paces.

"How was I to know, for Pete's sake?"

"I gave you a list of all the crew members," he returned, fully as heatedly as she. "This Wilson just happens to be the leader of our run."

"Theodore Wilson? There was no Theodore Wilson on that list." Andy frowned, creasing her brow. "Not that it matters, anyway. The point is, what are we going to do?"

"Do?" All the air of having confronted an escaped lunatic was packed tightly into that one small word. "We are going to get on a raft and run down the Colorado River, that's what."

"But—"

"Andy, be reasonable. It's too late to back out. We'll

just stay out of the lead raft and away from him as much as possible. If he bothers you, we'll threaten him with legal action for harassment. Okay? Now, quit worrying. Remember, you've got me here to protect you."

It was cold comfort, but Andra did not resist when he drew her back toward the others. She knew he was right. It was too late to leave. If they all behaved like adults, there might be nothing more than some slight awkwardness over this. After all, it was over and done with more than two years ago! But that thought didn't comfort her either.

She put on the ugly, wide-brimmed hat with chin strap which Rick handed her, grateful that it would shadow any expression to be found in her wide, nut-brown eyes. Andy was certain she didn't want anyone to read what she was thinking. The thoughts pricked by the sight of Theodore Wilson weren't pleasant.

Carol Wilson's divorce had been the kind of case Andra couldn't help getting personally involved in, with disastrous results. He'd contested the divorce, dragging the process out inch by inch, month by month, until Carol nearly suffered a breakdown. Against her better judgment, Andy had provided the shoulder for Carol to lean on, even taking her home to stay for a couple of weeks. Which had led to the incident that was causing her to tremble as she stood beside Rick. Only too vividly, she recalled the night Wilson appeared at her door, drunkenly demanding his wife be handed over to him.

Like a parcel of goods from a shop, thought Andy, her blood heating at the memory. She moved automatically with the group toward the launching site where the rafts would be lifted one by one into the water to glide off into the deep gorge. The boatman with the earring demonstrated the fastenings on the life jackets while Wilson issued a reminder that they were required to wear the jackets at all times on the water. He then began directing the launch operation. Andra watched him, but in her mind's eye she saw him in the midst of an image she'd striven hard to erase.

He'd been darker blond then, with skin so pale it had gleamed in the dim cast of her hall light. Swaying slightly, Wilson had shoved her door wide before she could step away, catching the edge of her shoulder and knocking her awry. She'd exaggerated when she told Rick he'd ransacked her apartment. After staggering through the few rooms and not finding Carol in any of them, he'd released his frustrated fury on her bookshelf, pulling it from the wall to send it crashing to the carpet, spraying books and ornaments across her living room. Horrified, Andy had pivoted, prepared to dash into her bedroom and call the police. The first sob had halted her in mid-step; the second had caused her to turn and stare with disbelieving eyes as Wilson knelt beside the tumbled disarray, shoulders bowed and head in hands.

Unconsciously, Andy's fingers clenched at the recollection. She heard a smothered curse and looked down to see her long nails digging deep into Rick's arm.

"I'm sorry," she said, detaching her fingers from his skin. But her apology was mechanical; her thoughts lingered in the past, where she saw herself slipping into her bedroom, leaving Wilson alone with his despair. When she came out the next morning, he was gone. He ceased fighting the proceedings after that, and she'd seen him only once more, grim and silent in court when Carol Wilson was granted her divorce. Andy had pressed no charges against him for his actions that night in her apartment, but she doubted he'd be grateful about that. In all probability he would dislike her all the more.

Ho, boy, this was going to be some rotten vacation, she sighed to herself. The first raft was lifted into the river. She turned to tell Rick to hold back until the last raft was put in, but a forceful hand thrust against the small of her back, shoving her forward with her words sputtering uselessly from her lips. The shock of extremely cold water swallowing her feet woke her to the realization that she was being propelled into the lead raft. A voice shrilled in her ear, calling out Rick's name, and she was surprised when he climbed into the bobbing rubber beside her.

"Don't worry. I'm here with you," he said, as if responding to something she'd said. "Hold on to the loose gear straps if you're frightened."

Because the river was quite calm here, she was able to hold on with a modicum of bravery, but her heart continued to hurl itself into her ribs as she struggled to avoid looking at the back of the oarsman seating himself directly before her. She focused on the cliffs rising beyond the slender expansion of the Navajo Bridge. As they passed beneath it, Andra bent her neck back to stare upward at the colossal towers of cream, buff, white, red, and maroon which blended mystically together to form Marble Canyon. But when her gaze fell, she found herself unable to look at anything beyond the undulation of arm and back muscles as Wilson easily maneuvered the raft down sun-sparkled water.

Andy forced herself to look beyond him to the other two passengers seated at the front of the craft. She vaguely thought the pert brunette had been introduced as Karla and the slim, serious bushy-haired boy as Brent. It could only have been Wilson who shoved her into this raft, but she didn't know why. An absurd panic rose within her that had nothing to do with being on the water. The only way back to civilization was fourteen days down the Grand Canyon with a man who had good reason to resent her.

Knotting her hands together, she chanced a sidelong look at Wilson as he rowed and was disconcerted to find him eyeing her over his shoulder. His gray eyes narrowed in cautious appraisal of her, as if he expected her to jump overboard at any moment. He frowned briefly at her. Her chin went up defiantly and he returned his attention to the river ahead.

Brent twisted round to ask of Wilson, "How rough a rapids is Badger Creek?" It was a question Andy would have been happy not to have heard asked. She was remembering her fear of drowning.

"Intermediate. A rating of 4 to 6," he replied shortly. "It varies depending on the river flow. When the water is high, the rapids are generally easier."

Rick promptly explained to Andy that the rapids were rated according to a scale similar to the Richter scale for earthquakes. On the Western scale, a rating of 1 meant nothing more than a riffle, while 10 denoted a rapid was "not recommended." She longed to tell him she'd rather not know, thank you very much, but visions of that cautious appraisal and brief frown kept her from speaking. It was apparent Wilson expected her to panic, and she vowed not to give him the satisfaction of being right.

The first warning was a low growling. Straining to see ahead, Andra saw a smooth pool bounded by sandbanks covered with clumps of willow and tamarisk. A curling wave leapt above the edge of the pool. Her mouth went dry. Her breath caught as Wilson stood, checked their position, then sat and pulled sharply on the oars. Before she had time to voice her alarm, they were past the pool and into the increased roar of the rapids. With her eyes squeezed tightly shut, Andy felt a torrent of cold water wash over her amidst a series of roller-coasterlike joltings for maybe thirty seconds. When she pried open her eyes, she discovered they were already safely out. She looked down to see herself thoroughly splattered, then up to see Wilson's eyes narrowly scan the damp cotton of her blouse clinging to her breasts.

She tightly wound her fingers together, fighting the urge to hide behind her hands. It was absurd, totally absurd, for her heart to continue clamoring so loudly. The rapids had been passed; they were out of danger. But as she saw the sun strike silver in the hair of the man before her, she unreasonably felt more in danger than ever.

Water splashed with merry plops as people abandoned the rafts, ready to pull them onto a sandy beach strewn with boulders and shrubs. As Andy climbed out, her knees were shaking slightly, but whether this was due to Badger Creek Rapids or Wilson's gloved hand at her elbow as he steered her out of the shallow water, she couldn't say. He left almost instantly to oversee the heaving of their rafts ashore, and in all the general camp activity of unloading and unpacking, she didn't have time to worry over which had unsettled her more.

A metal box grill was set up onshore, and several people scattered to gather driftwood for the fire. Others were directed to collect water, which would be chemically purified for them to drink. Food packs and other gear were lifted from the rafts. Andy stood immobile, feeling uncomfortably useless. A heavy canvas duffel smacked into her legs, almost knocking her off balance.

"Come on," said Rick, carrying his own bag and their sleeping gear to a slightly secluded spot away from the main camp. After a moment's hesitation, Andy pulled on her bag and proceeded to follow him.

Thirty pounds had seemed an incredible minimum for her personal gear when she'd packed back home in Kansas City. Dragging her duffel bag through the sand in Rick's wake, Andy discovered it was considerably more gear than she wanted. She stumbled, saw the lace of her wet tennis shoe dangling, and knelt to retie it.

When she looked up, she saw Wilson standing across a stretch of sand. Without the life jacket, she could see just how magnificently muscled his chest actually was. The sun flashed over his incredibly blond hair, almost blinding her. She knew, however, that his gaze was fixed on her.

Her hand shook. Someone called "Tif," and he turned away. She forced herself to stand up and pull her bag to where Rick was spreading their sleeping rolls near a feathery cluster of tamarisks.

"I thought we agreed to stay out of the lead raft," he said a shade too dryly as she neared.

"But I didn't—" she started to protest, then shrugged. Andra wasn't the woman to waste time in useless argument. "Anyway, I found out why we didn't know who our fearless leader was." She plopped her duffel bag beside his, then tore off her water-speckled hat and cast it into the sand. Squatting down, she combed her long fingers through her short disarray of hair. "He's called Tif, not Theodore or Ted. How was I to know who Tif Wilson would turn out to be?"

"Well, he seems to be leaving you alone," responded Rick distractedly. He sat on his heels and began rifling through the contents in his duffel. "Maybe he doesn't remember you."

Her glare of disgust withered this suggestion before it could blossom. "Don't be a total idiot. But if we just stay out of each other's way, I think it'll be okay."

"Good," he mumbled, obviously not paying the least attention. Grinning, he extracted a waterproof pouch from the depths of his bag. He doffed this pouch to release his camera. "Hey, Andy, smile," he ordered as he snapped her, arms akimbo, scowling fiercely at him. He moved off to aim his lens left, then right, and with a sigh, Andra began stuffing his gear haphazardly back into his bag.

The seed of hope had been planted. Perhaps Wilson didn't recall who she was. After all, she didn't look like the same person without the linen suits and the stylish makeup. And her hair was a total mess, not the least like her usual carefully curled coiffure. Perhaps if she stayed as far away from him as possible, he wouldn't remember.

"That's no way to pack gear," said a gravelly voice behind her, sending her about three feet into the air.

All hope that Tif Wilson had forgotten her died before she turned around. He may have become more tanned, more blond, more muscularly fit, but his voice was as full of contempt as ever.

She continued blindly jamming clothes into Rick's bag, telling herself to remain calm. Without warning she was yanked away from the duffel bag and pushed back into the sand.

"Here. Let me show you." He began efficiently folding and stowing as if by rote. When he'd jerked the drawstrings together and dropped the bag beside her, he looked down into her distressed gaze. "What are you doing here?"

"What do you mean?"

"Just what I asked."

The nearby rapids echoed his tone, a sort of hard rumbling that somehow soothed and startled at the same time. She tried to read his meaning from his countenance but gave it up. His face might as well have been one of the ancient canyon rocks for all the expression to be seen there.

Feeling at a distinct disadvantage as he towered over her, Andra scrambled to her feet. Even upright she remained at a disadvantage, the top of her head only reaching his chin. To cover the shaking in her limbs, she wiped grits of sand from her jeans. "I might ask you that. As I recall, you were something far from a river raft runner—a professor, weren't you?"

"Mathematics," he confirmed with a nod. "Still am. I just do this to keep fit during the summers. And you? You still a courtroom pettifogger?"

Andra stiffened. There was no mistaking the animosity in that insult. She opened her mouth to tell him to take a flying leap into the river, then abruptly shut it again. It would do little good to argue the length of the Colorado River. One of them had to make the effort to approach this in an adult manner.

"I'm still a member of the bar," she said flatly. "I'm here on vacation and nothing more. I had no idea you were the leader of this group until I saw you in Lee's Ferry."

"You here with your . . . friend?" With great deliberation he avoided looking at her sleeping bag laid out so neatly beside another.

"Yes," she answered, tipping her chin up. How dare he sneer at her like that! What she did or didn't do was no concern of his. He had no right to question why she was here or with whom. She saw no reason to explain that her friend was just that, nothing more. In a precise, passionless tone she stated, "Rick's a partner at Colbern, Hanks."

The mention of her law firm affected him like a slap. He winced and jerked slightly away. Seeing this, Andy paused, glancing down at the sand sprinkled over her tennies. Two years and more may have passed since his divorce, but it was obvious Wilson had not gotten over it. When she raised her eyes she knew a moment of palpable dismay. He was eyeing her with the look of a man who found the sight before him distasteful. She sucked in a deep breath of courage.

"As we're pretty much stuck in this situation, I suggest we make the best of it. I'll stay out of your way, and you can pretend I'm not even here."

His gaze settled over her like cold ashes left from a long-dead fire. "I haven't got that good of an imagination."

She shifted her eyes away from the look that was making her feel chilled despite the inner canyon heat. The pounding, seething, hissing, of the rapids behind them seemed to ricochet off their stretched silence.

"Carol," muttered Tif at last.

Startled, Andra stared straight at him. To her astonishment, a deep stain darkened the tan on his cheeks.

"Do you ever see her?" he inquired, his voice stronger.

"Why, no. Don't you know? She moved out of Kansas City—"

"How the hell should I know what she's done?" he cut in with a sudden flash of angry pain. "*You* helped to strip me of that right!"

Before she could think of a response, any response, to this bitter accusation, an arm draped over her shoulder.

In a carefully neutral tone, Rick asked, "How's it going? You got us ready for the night, babe?"

"Uh . . . Tif, this is Rick," said Andy after an unaccountably embarrassed hesitation.

"Your friend," said Tif blandly, all anger seemingly gone. He directed a short nod at Rick, but the gesture was clearly dismissive. It signaled that they were not going to be friends.

Andy nipped furiously at her lower lip. As expected, Wilson was behaving like an uncivilized barbarian. Didn't he know this simply wasn't how divorces were taken these days? She silently fumed, wanting to tell him that it wasn't her fault Carol left him, that she'd just done her job, but she knew he'd simply resent her even more. It occurred to her that Rick's trip could be ruined because of this idiot's warped hostility toward her. The thought overrode her rising temper with a rational need for calm. She must do nothing to further inflame the embers of ill will; she must do nothing to make this trip any worse than it already was going to be.

"That's right," she said on a falsely bright note. She plastered a smile into place and added, "He's not a turkey like I am, so you won't have him getting underfoot."

"And you? Will you be getting underfoot?" inquired Wilson with that disconcerting cold gaze.

"Of course not. I already told you I'll keep out of your

way." By dint of a tremendous effort, Andy kept that smile fastened on her lips, but she yearned to childishly kick his shin and stick out her tongue at him.

"Just see that you do," he returned, then spun on his heel and went back to the campfire.

"Sorry I didn't see that he was bothering you sooner, Andy. I got hung up taking pictures," explained Rick with an apologetic smile.

"That's okay," said Andra, but as usual, Rick wasn't listening. He was already sauntering away to point his camera at another of the colorful wedges of rock surrounding them.

She didn't mind. Being left alone to her thoughts suited her to a T. It appeared that Wilson meant to take out all his antagonistic feelings about his divorce on her. Though such a deep chasm of anger after so long a time would have surprised her in any other man, it really didn't do so in Theodore Wilson. Since he'd come to her apartment that night and revealed his soul, Andra had known he loved Carol with an enduring passion.

What she didn't know was why she should suddenly feel so depressed about it.

CHAPTER TWO

A sea of vermilion dusk flooded the campsite. The magical splendor of the sun's glittering descent held them breathless the moment before the crisp edge of night crept in upon them. Andra looked at the circle of firelit faces, listened to the hushed murmuring of voices, and felt a rich contentment. She was lazily sated after a tremendous feast of grilled steak and foil-wrapped corn on the cob; it added to the upswelling of satisfaction she was experiencing.

"Didn't I tell you this would be great?" whispered Rick in her right ear.

Smiling, she nodded. "You were right. It's wonderful."

She turned her head to throw her smile up at him. It was captured instead by Tif, sitting just beyond the circle of campers. He was staring at her as if they were intimately isolated instead of surrounded by twenty-three other people. Shivering, Andra's contentment vanished. If he had reached out and touched her, she knew she couldn't possibly have responded more quickly—her breath, pulse, senses, all stirred on the brief stroke of his gaze. Distress over her incredible reaction couldn't dim the brilliant flash of desire which burst through her.

Even as her smile faded, Andy knew she must have imagined that look, that it must have been some trick of the flickering fire flames. In the instant before Tif shifted his attention, his expression was quite blank.

Long practice in suppressing her emotions with a neutral self-control for courtroom performances enabled her to address Rick, to respond when Karla spoke to her, to smile at others. It was only in her innermost depths that Andy's violent turmoil was revealed. There she chided herself for being so disconcerted by a mere glance. There she told herself it had been anxiety that Wilson would cause a scene that had disturbed her, nothing more.

Half-listening to Brent tell Rick about a trip he'd taken down the Green River, half-berating herself for her foolish reactions, Andy didn't hear Tif approach. A bowl seemed to appear out of nowhere and her hands automatically wrapped around it.

"Come help me get water for washing up," he said. It was a point-blank command, but Andra suspected she'd have followed him anyway.

She stood and shrugged apologetically at Rick, then hurried down the beach after Tif's striding form. Why had he chosen her to do this? It could only be that he wanted to talk. Andy wasn't sure she was ready for another round with him, especially after that unbelievable tumult of feeling she'd experienced. Yet she never seriously considered turning around and handing the bowl to someone else. Maybe she could convince him that they could get through this in a mature, civilized manner. Don't be stupid, she instantly snapped at herself. This man doesn't know what civilized manners are! By the time she caught up with him at water's edge, her heart was galloping in apprehensive anticipation.

A curtain of shadows veiled them, though silvery glints of Tif's hair could be seen as he moved. The loose tails of the shirt he'd donned when the sun went down flared darkly as he knelt and scooped water into each of the bowls he'd carried. Andy fervently wished that she could see his face so she could gauge his thoughts as she did so often with witnesses.

"This your first wilderness trip?" he asked.

The tranquillity of his tone matched that of the esoteric gorge surrounding them. Andra had always associated his deep voice with an iron steam of anger, rumbling hotly like some runaway freight train, and this unexpected placidity surprised her. Cautiously, hesitant to believe in his goodwill, yet fearing not to, she replied lightly, "It shows, huh? To me, any area not bounded by concrete constitutes wilderness."

His low chuckle blended into the endless gurgling of the rapids above. "There's nothing like starting out on a—if you'll pardon the pun—grand scale. So how did you like your first run on a raft?"

"Well . . . I think I was too scared to *like* it," she admitted with a rueful laugh.

"Good. Fear will keep you careful on the river. Not that rafting's as hazardous as most people think. It's true there's risk, there's always a struggle with the water, but the danger isn't as great as that of driving on a freeway. But if you stay scared, you stay cautious."

"You don't need to worry about me—I can assure you I'll stay good and scared! I've been wondering all day how I let Rick talk me into this."

"He's a lawyer, isn't he?" returned Tif, his voice hardening. "Like any good counselor, I'm sure he's learned the fine art of manipulation."

"Oh." Andy tensed, her breath huffed into the night. His almost friendly manner had effectively drawn her off guard. When his first jab came, she'd no longer been prepared. She recovered nearly immediately. "Whatever you have against me, please don't take it out on Rick. He's done nothing to you, and just because he's with me is no reason to spoil his vacation."

The spectral flash of his hair as his head tilted was all she could see, but she could hear the taut resentment in his reply.

"I'm not taking anything out on anyone. I just stated a fact."

"Fact? What fact? You've no reason to generalize about lawyers being manipulative."

"No reason?" His incredulity was plain.

Andy knew this was the time to strip off the white gloves. "No reason," she repeated firmly. "Carol wasn't manipulated by anyone, least of all by me. If I'd had my way, she'd have taken far more than she ever did—she bent over backwards to be generous to you in the settlement. The division of your property—"

"Settlement! Property!" interrupted Tif sharply. "That's all you damned attorneys can think of, isn't it? You think that getting a better deal on the alimony payment should make me happy, is that it?" He let out a string of expletives that blistered Andy's ears, then jerked to his feet and stalked back toward the campsite.

After several stunned seconds, she slopped water into her bowl and slowly followed him, wondering how she was going to convince him they could get along for the next two weeks. She'd thought, briefly, that he'd realized this—he'd started out friendly enough tonight. Going back over their conversation, Andy wished she'd ignored his comments about lawyers. She knew he had reason enough to resent the profession and scolded herself for not having more understanding. She remembered his roughly soothing voice, his deep chuckle, and strongly felt she should rip out her tongue. The loss of her opportunity to smooth things over made her want to scream with frustration; the intensity of her feelings upset her even more, and she approached the ring of people in a mood of angry self-reproach.

"From now on you'll each collect your own water for personal washing," Tif was saying as she drew near. "When you're done, dump the residue at least one hundred feet from the river, well above the water."

"What about bathing?" called out a faceless voice.

"As we move downriver there are temperate pools for swimming and bathing, using biodegradable soap. But don't attempt it in the Colorado itself. The current is hazardous, and the temperature is too cold. The dangers of drowning and of hypothermia are very real."

Without acknowledging her in any way, Tif turned and took the water bowl from her hands. He handed her two empty bowls in return and strode off toward the river. Andra stared down at the bowls in her hands, up at his receding silhouette, then stumbled down the beach in his wake. He didn't break his stride nor turn to see if she followed. Upon reaching the river edge, he stood waiting, a stiff, silent outline of black against night's opaque backdrop.

"I'm sorry," he said the moment she came up beside him.

The blunt apology left her speechless. From what she'd seen of him before and from all the horror stories Carol had related, Andy had expected Tif to lose his white-hot temper easily and often. What she hadn't expected was for him to apologize about it—Carol Wilson had made his inflexibility very clear. She sought for the words to form her own apology, but he didn't give her the chance to say them.

"What I really wanted to ask about," he said, still without looking at her, "was Carol. Since I send the alimony checks to your firm, I've had no contact with her at all." He hesitated, then explained flatly, "I'd like to know how she's doing."

Andy swallowed. She was surprised to find that it hurt to do so. Finally, she forced out, "I . . . um, well, that is—"

"Did she ask you not to tell me?" His low voice grated harshly.

"No, of course not. She didn't know I'd see you again. But . . . are you sure you want to know?" Even as she asked, she wondered why she longed to shield him from more pain.

He was silent for a long moment. Then he bent down to fill the bowls. "You ever had a toothache? You know if you play your tongue against that tooth it's going to hurt. But you do it anyway. You can't resist. That's how it is with Carol. I can't resist wanting to know what she's doing, how she is, even though I know damn well it's going to hurt to find out."

An oppressive weight seemed to sink right down to her sneakers, but somehow Andra managed to keep her voice level. "Carol's in Dallas, working as program director for one of the TV stations there. She loves it." Andy kept her eyes fixed on her two bowls of water. Even hidden by layers of night shadows, she didn't want to face Tif when she went on. "And she wrote that she's . . . thinking of getting married again."

Braced for an outburst, Andy waited breathlessly for his explosion. Finally, unable to restrain herself any longer, she twisted around to face him. He perched on his heels, motionless, gazing out over the river. She ached to comfort him but sensed his need to make his own peace with this news. Minute added to minute and still he sat, locked in his own thoughts. It seemed to Andra that he'd become a part of the austere beauty around them, that he shared the immobile serenity of the harsh canyon.

Suddenly he rose, his blond hair a beacon of his movement. She saw him glance down at her, then away. "You'll have to be faster than this with bailing buckets on the raft," he remarked tonelessly before leaving.

Once again Andy was left staring at his back until shaking herself into following him. Each step she took was measured, as if trying to count out her mental review of the bits and pieces which formed Tif Wilson. He was, she decided, the most incomprehensible man she'd ever met. From what she had known of him, she hadn't expected such a mild acceptance of her bombshell news. In a way she almost wished he *had* blown up. That would have fit in with her image of him; his quiet settling with himself had forever changed that image.

What, after all, did she really know of him? When she'd known him before, she'd seen only a partial view, a profile that had been painted for her by Carol. Admittedly, Carol's view was biased. Andra realized she'd never taken the time to examine the full portrait of the man. Perhaps, after all, he wasn't quite the domineering, unreasonably explosive man she'd believed him to be.

Her heart did a curious flip at the thought. Her nerves oddly danced. As they had all day, Andy's reactions staggered her. She didn't want to react to Tif Wilson at all, much less in this inexplicably breathless way. It must surely be all the excitement of starting this trip. By morning she would certainly be her usual sane, sensible self. With this thought in mind, Andy decided to head directly to bed.

Keeping one of the bowls she'd collected, she retreated to the relative seclusion behind a clump of tamarisks where her gear lay spread out. After she washed her face and brushed her teeth, she stood indecisively nibbling on her lower lip, wondering what to do about undressing. She'd never thought of herself as overly modest, but the notion of stripping down in front of twenty-four strangers, most of them male, was somewhat daunting.

"Hey, Andy," called Rick, interrupting her ruminations. He was waving her toward the now-dying driftwood fire. "Come over here. Tif's got some stuff to tell us."

Relieved to put the entire matter of undressing off for the time being, she obeyed Rick's signal. As she drew near, she saw Tif standing quietly at ease with his thumbs hooked into the pockets of his cutoffs while everyone gathered around him. Casually, effortlessly he exuded a strength, an aura of authority that Andy had to admire. Then he began, completely ruining her sense of security.

"Before we go any further, you need to face some realities about life here in the canyon," said Tif with a circling glance which encompassed the entire assemblage. His words had a grim, ominous ring that Andra definitely didn't like. As he spoke about care of the camp and use of the portable toilets, however, she relaxed. He moved on to cactus, loose rocks, whirlpools, and rattlesnakes. She mentally moaned. He began explaining what to do if a raft flipped over. She stood rigidly, longing intensely to wring his neck. Why didn't he give this speech back in Lee's Ferry where she'd still had a chance to escape?

The group was dissolving, some back toward the dying fire, some toward bedrolls. Tif halted them with a raised hand.

"One last thing. Some of you have already spread out your sleeping bags. From now on, roll bags out just as you bed down and not before." He paused to let this sink in, then went on. "Those of you who have unrolled your bags check them carefully before you get in. Scorpions have a habit of crawling into anything left lying open."

A babble broke out, highlighted by a few high squeaks. Andy felt her color drain away and thought she would faint. Spiders of any kind terrified her; the thought of a scorpion in her bag made her feel sick. Clutching at the first support she could find, which turned out to be Rick's arm, she stammered, "I—I'll never be able to get into that b-bag."

"Don't worry about your bag, darlin'," returned Rick

with a suggestive quirk of his overfull lips. "We'll just zip ours together, and I'll keep the scorpions off you."

She ignored the teasing leer. It didn't fool her in the least. She knew that if she agreed to sleep in his bag, Rick would run screaming up the canyon walls. He liked to play at flirting with her—mostly, she thought, out of habit—but the last thing he wanted was to be taken seriously. Having been hired on at Colbern, Hanks at the same time, the two newest, most junior partners had naturally gravitated toward one another, but there'd never been any substance to the light flirtation which underscored their friendship.

"Why didn't you tell me about the scorpions before you dragged me here?" she demanded hotly, fear touching off her anger. She flung an arm out for emphasis, striking a solid wall of musculature. Whirling with her mixture of fright and fury clear upon her face, Andy found herself facing Tif. It was at once apparent that he'd heard the whole exchange; his eyes swept contemptuously over her. Numbly she realized he must think poorly of anyone upset by such a paltry thing as sleeping with a scorpion, but she had no opportunity to explain her fears before he once again focused his attention on the entire group.

"There's no reason to be scared," said Tif softly, yet so firmly all jabbering ceased. "A scorpion's sting is rarely fatal, and we've got a well-stocked medical kit. But as with everything else in the wilderness, it's just as well to be cautious. Check your bags thoroughly before getting in and shake out your shoes before putting them on in the morning."

He swiveled and moved away, signaling the end of the discussion. Andra hardly noticed. *Rarely* fatal, the man said. That meant occasionally they were. She was trembling, unable to think as Rick steered her back to their bedding-down spot. *What am I doing here?* she asked herself repeatedly.

"Buck up, Andy," said Rick. His voice was tinged with impatience, but there was kindness in it as well. "He has to tell us all that crap. He has to tell us about the scorpions and the snakes just like the stewardesses on a plane have to show us the oxygen masks. Now if you like, you can share my bag tonight."

This time his proposal lacked the suggestiveness he'd used earlier. He offered his protection, as one might offer to sleep with a child afraid of the dark. The image of a scorpion crawling over her while she was asleep and vulnerable settled all questions of propriety or modesty.

"Oh, Rick, thanks," she sighed with relief.

"I'll take care of your bag," stated someone behind them.

Both jumped slightly, for they'd not been aware of Tif following them. For a stunned second neither said a word, then as Tif quickly knelt to unzip, examine, and shake out Andy's empty sleeping bag, Rick started forward.

"That won't be necessary. I can take care of—"

"Look, the whole purpose of taking a trip like this is to understand and become part of nature," interrupted Tif. "Andra's here to learn to appreciate the violent beauty of the wilderness, not to be afraid of it. If you have to constantly 'protect' her from experiencing the spirit of natural danger, she might as well not be here at all. She might as well be sitting in her cushy office back in K.C."

Hearing the intensity of his voice, Andy's heart plummeted. He *did* think her a coward—for which he blatantly had little time and less respect. She shouldn't give a damn what he thought, she knew that, yet she had to admit she did. Without reason, she cared terribly. And it was this need for his good opinion that led her to tamp down her fright. Her lips split in what she was certain was a ghoulish parody of a smile.

"Tif's right," she said. Surprisingly, her voice was level. "I can call out if—if something"—she couldn't bring herself to say "if scorpions"—"should get in my bag. I still don't know what I'm doing here, but since I am here, I might as well try to get into the spirit of things."

She was rewarded with a genuine flash of approval from Tif and a lightweight scowl from Rick. The latter's frown was marred by his evident relief, and Andy's fear dissipated in a desire to laugh. Womanizing, swinging Rick Paisley was relieved not to have to cuddle up to a warm, feminine body for the night! She wasn't sure she shouldn't be insulted, but it was so amusing that a true smile replaced the artificial one on her lips.

"But you're here because of me," protested Rick somewhat halfheartedly. "It's up to me to watch out for you."

That explained the frown. His male ego was bruised. Andra knew how to salve his pride. She said softly, "You have, Rick, and I hope you'll continue to. It's just that I agree I should try to blend in. If I don't, I'll ruin both our vacations."

"I suggest you begin your blending by getting into your bag for the night," Tif said in a dry, harsh tone. "Dawn comes early in the canyon."

Rick deliberately moved some feet away to shake out his own bag, leaving Andy to gape at Tif. From approving her feeble gesture of bravery, Wilson had swiftly returned to his earlier disparaging attitude. An overwhelming resentment shook her. She'd tried to be pleasant, she'd tried to be brave, and this big lug didn't appreciate a lick of all her effort!

With a grand wave of her hand, she indicated the expanse of rocks and sand while infusing her voice with all the disdain she could manage. "Oh? And just where do you suggest I change? Or do you suggest I sleep in my clothes?"

His pale brows rose infinitesimally, and the downward curve of his narrow eyes seemed to deepen. Inching his gaze over her, he reviewed the uncombed tumult of her brown hair, the pale glow of her skin, and the curves of her shapely silhouette. The heat of his lingering gaze seemed to melt the clothes from her figure, exposing Andy as surely as if he'd removed her shirt and jeans. Involuntarily, she took a step back.

He glanced back up at her face. He rubbed a tanned finger over the crook on his nose, then dropped it to slide along the curve of his lip. "No, I'd certainly not suggest that. By all means, take off your clothes."

The patent note of sensuality, the hint of sexual intimacy in his gesture, dumfounded her. Whatever she'd been expecting from him—antagonism, resentment, even resigned acceptance—it hadn't been *this*. The shock numbed her own erratic feelings. Without pausing to think, needing to say something, anything to break this spell, she stammered out, "B-but where?"

His chuckle had been pleasant, soothing. His laughter was a charge of enjoyment. "You've nothing to be ashamed of, believe me," he said when he could. Then he paused, and all laughter faded from his voice. "Or to fear, either. But if modesty insists, you change in your bag."

"It's not a matter of modesty," she promptly contradicted, wanting this exchange to go on, wanting to hear his marvelous laughter again.

"No? What then?"

"Privacy," she answered smugly.

"Next trip we'll pack your private dressing room, Andy," put in Rick as he came toward them. He cast a conspiratorial wink at Tif. "And we'll put in the four-poster to go with it."

"Don't forget the TV and the maid," added Tif.

"Okay, okay," Andy laughed, putting up both hands defensively. "I'm sorry I brought it up. I'll make do with the bag."

"Hell, who needs a bag?" Rick grinned broadly and began to undo the buttons of his shirt with all the flair of an accomplished stripper. He turned, wiggled his hips provocatively, and let the shirt slide off his shoulders. Andy's smile of appreciation expanded when his hand moved to the zipper on his jeans. She knew he wouldn't dare.

"Your modesty has a double standard," remarked Tif, drawing her eyes from Rick's show. She blinked at him, not understanding at first because she knew full well the performance would fall off long before those jeans did. He tipped his head slightly toward the retreating Rick. "You seemed to be getting the most out of his immodesty."

"He's just teasing. He's one big tease," she said, raising her voice so Rick would hear.

"You're just jealous," he called back, " 'cuz I put on a better show!"

Before she could protest this bit of slander, Tif lightly grazed her cheek with his fingertip, garnering her complete attention. The touch was mercurial, gone almost as soon as she'd felt it. Andy's awareness of it, however, intensified as her adrenaline began pumping at an alarming rate.

"He's not your lover," he murmured.

It sounded like a thought mistakenly spoken, but she replied as if it had been a question. "No, of course not."

"Do you want him to be? Is that why you came with him?"

If any other man had asked her such an outrageous question, Andra would have told him in no uncertain terms to mind his own business. Now she simply caught her breath and said seriously, "No. We're friends and neither of us wants it any other way."

"Good," returned Tif softly.

Not for the first time that night she cursed the heavy darkness which hid his expression from her. She sensed his satisfaction, his easing stance, but she wanted to know why he should suddenly relax. Could it possibly have been the presence of Rick and not her fear of scorpions that engendered his earlier disapproval? Absurdly, her heart leapt at the notion.

"Why should you ask such a thing?" she queried.

"Wait a minute," he responded obliquely.

With his swift, silent stride, he left her to consider what had just occurred between them. Or had anything happened at all? Had she imagined it all, feeding the flames of excitement in his eyes with the kindling of her own totally unexpected, unwanted desires? A thoroughly unreasonable hostility at that possibility set a faint frown on her face, pressing the crease into place in her brow. Of all the things she didn't need to complicate her life, a holiday affair with a man as stable as a load of nitroglycerine was first on the list.

She pressed her hand against her cheek, trapping the ghost of his brief touch. A disturbing quiver at the memory disquieted her, and she jerked her hand away from her face. It would be madness! In addition to having a temper that was always loaded and primed, Tif Wilson was incredibly possessive and definitely chauvinistic. How many times had she listened to Carol complain of his jealousy, of his attempts to subvert her career and keep her at home? No, she didn't want to get involved—physically or otherwise—with this man.

Having successfully talked herself out of any foolish impulses, Andy sat atop her sleeping bag and pulled off her tennis shoes. She briefly considered putting them inside the bag with her, thereby reducing the chance of finding any morning callers within them, but decided not to give anyone any further opportunity to make fun of her. She was about to crawl inside when Tif abruptly appeared before her, eliciting a startled squawk.

His habit of unearthly movement compounded his ability to disconcert her, and Andy gave rein to her annoyance.

"Must you always sneak around like that?" she demanded on a snap.

"Sorry. I didn't mean to scare you," he said quietly. "I told you to wait, I was coming back."

Seeing that he held a sleeping roll under one arm and a canvas duffel in the other, she didn't attempt to argue this point. Instead, she asked directly, "What are you doing?"

"Preparing to bed down for the night." He dropped both roll and bag and began to spread his gear out next to hers.

"But you can't—"

"Why not?"

Andra bit her lip, wishing she'd learn to keep her mouth shut. He could, of course, sleep just where he pleased. What bothered her was not that he chose to sleep near her, but *why* he chose to do so. She both longed and feared to know the answer. Shrugging, she said nonchalantly, "No reason."

He reached into his bag and drew out a T-shirt. "Here. You can use this as a nightshirt. Should fit just about right," he summed up as his eyes did another quick calculation of her figure.

She stared at the slate-gray cloth as if it might sprout fangs and bite her. "Oh, that's okay, I don't need—" she began, but dimly seeing the amusement she sensed he was feeling, she broke off and mutely took it from his outstretched hand. She zipped up her sleeping bag, then wriggled gingerly into it, submerging her entire body. Twisting and turning in a series of unique contortions, she discarded her clothes and maneuvered herself into her "nightshirt." The fit could have been described as overwhelming, but since no one was in her bag to view it, Andy simply snuggled within its ample folds to sleep.

It was surprisingly warm. Too warm. After several minutes she was forced to stick her head out, followed by an arm.

"I wondered when you'd come up for air," rumbled that deep voice she was rapidly learning to associate with amusement, not anger.

"Mummph," she responded, rolling onto her side and into the too-warm confines of the bag.

The zipper was undone and the top cover flung outward. Her protest was never uttered. As soon as Andy felt the night air caress her, a thin sheet was spread over her. She sat up.

"Lie down and go to sleep," ordered Tif, pressing her back down and speaking as if she were twenty years younger. "You'd roast if you tried to sleep inside your bag. It rarely gets below sixty-five at night here. As the temperatures drop during the night, you can always pull the top back over you if you get cold."

"But—but the bugs and—and things," she objected anxiously, "they'll get on me."

"Shut up and go to sleep" was all he said, but his command was softened by a gentle warmth Andra really couldn't fight.

She lay back. Sleep, huh! That proved how little *he* knew! Between worrying over Tif Wilson and stray scorpions—and really, was there much difference between the two?—she knew she'd never get a moment's rest.

What, she demanded of herself for the hundredth time that day, *am I doing here?*

CHAPTER THREE

As dawn drifted into the camp she awoke with a lazy stretch, tangled within sheet, sleeping bag, and half-remembered dreams. Her flash of fearful disorientation was instantaneously lulled by the complex pulsating jumble of hisses, clanks, and poundings distantly echoing from the rapids. Without thinking, she threw her covers back, stretched again, and sat up.

"I knew that would look a hell of a lot better on you than it ever did on me," drawled Tif.

Her head whirled around. His long form lay sideways across the top of his bag, head propped on one arm as he watched her. He was already dressed in cutoffs and unbuttoned shirt, making Andy terribly conscious of just how close to her hips his T-shirt had risen in the night. Jerking the hem down, she threw one solid glare in his direction.

"Makes a delightful nightshirt," he added provocatively.

There was no way she could maintain the least amount of ire. His smile, his tone, his sleep-tousled hair, all captivated her; the blatant appreciation in his eyes mesmerized. Suddenly, she felt happy to be alive, happy to be precisely where she was. Stifling a girlish impulse to giggle, she reached behind and around, extracting her clothes from the jumble of her bed. A quick look at Tif proved to her that he was no gentleman. His gaze was firmly fastened on her. This, however, no longer annoyed her. It thrilled her in ways Andy had no wish to examine.

Thrusting any such unwanted questions aside, she stood, dug her bare toes into the soft sand, and cast her eyes over the campsite. Those who were stirring were far enough removed and too much occupied with themselves to take note of her. Looking behind her, she saw Rick's body immobile in the heavy stillness of a deep sleep. She returned her gaze to Tif's face. She watched him steadily as she stretched out a leg and very slowly began to draw on her jeans. He was most attentive, particularly when she finally ran up the zipper. Andra hesitated another moment, then caught the laughing challenge in those drowsy gray eyes. Facing him with a half smile of defiance, she yanked off the T-shirt in one swift motion.

His sharp intake of breath pierced the short distance separating them. As he leapt to his feet, Andy twirled and began hastily pulling on her bra and shirt. The instant she'd tugged the T-shirt off, she'd regretted it. She couldn't believe she'd had such an insane impulse, much less given in to it! God, what he must be thinking!

In her rush to get dressed, her fingers fumbled first with the front hook on the undergarment, then with the buttons on her top. He reached her long before she'd finished the operation. With fluid ease he spun her around and firmly took her fluttering hands in his. Circumventing her attempts to pull away, ignoring her mumbles of protest, he set her hands aside and calmly began to do up her buttons himself.

Her mind raced as her body went rigid. She was certain he could feel the frantic thumping of her heart, could hear the erratic rasp of her breath. What had possessed her to do such a thing? If only she could explain that she had never, would never, strip down for just anyone. If only she could explain the daring feeling, the impulse . . .

"What happened to modesty?" he inquired, slicing through her self-castigation. His mild teasing was so plainly clear of any condemnation that Andy's tense muscles relaxed.

"Modesty gave up trying to take a raft trip," she answered as flippantly as she could.

Immediately, she thought she'd mistaken the warmth in his voice. He was frowning at her, but she could feel a heat emanate from him that suggested something quite at odds with the disapproval shading his gray eyes and tightening his lips. "I don't know what got into me," she began, but he interrupted impatiently.

"Didn't you wear your hat yesterday?"

Mouth gaping open, Andy stared at him. She managed a nod of affirmation.

"Did you have any lotion on?"

This time she shook her head and he muttered. Telling her to wait, he strode off toward the main camp. She took one step after him but halted as she realized she had nothing on her feet. Disgruntled, she sat on her crumpled bed to wait. She wasn't about to touch her tennies until they'd been evicted of any possible inhabitants.

Hearing her name, Andy turned around to see Karla waving at her. A frenzied hand signal brought the brunette to her side, along with a shorter, plumpish blonde wearing a sleep-laden sulk.

"Mornin'," said Karla cheerfully. "This is Nancy Hartigan. Nancy, meet Andra James. If possible, we thought we'd pay a visit to the john at the same time and insure some privacy." She flapped the ends of a sheet which was draped over her shoulder.

This solution relieved Andra. Two portable chemical toilets had been carried ashore and set as far apart as possible, but even so, she'd had the feeling of being exposed whenever using one last night. "Sounds great, but would you mind checking out my shoes first?"

With a great deal of good-natured ribbing, Karla inspected the tennies before Andy stuffed her feet into them. She was glad to have something to think about other than Tif Wilson's lightning changes of mood and completely forgot his instructions to wait as she crossed the beach to the "ladies' room."

During the walk there and back, it became obvious to Andy that Karla wouldn't have bothered with a sheet, probably not with a toilet, if it hadn't been required by law. Her inhibitions—if she had any—were few. From her long, impudent streams of hair to her lithe figure, everything about Karla Lowe was casually, naturally unrepressed. She'd been on many such trips and spoke knowledgeably and with evident pleasure about rafting.

On the other hand, Nancy was, like Andra, a "turkey." Her lips pushed out in mute misery, except when they parted to emit a list of complaints which was, unfortunately, never-ending. She was appalled at the lack of conveniences—"Not even a radio, can you believe it?" she demanded of them. What to Andy and Karla had been a breathtaking, almost spiritual, setting of the sun the night before had been to Nancy a distressing dousing of light. By the time they reached the center of camp, where a steady flow of morning activity was occurring, Andy parted from the blonde with relief. She determined that no matter how rough things got, she'd keep her mouth shut. One whiner like Nancy was enough for any group.

One of the bearded oarsmen caught hold of Andy's arm and put her to work in the preparation of breakfast. Not exactly a luxury vacation, she thought with lighthearted cynicism as she helped dish out the eggs, sausage, hashbrowns, and toast that were cooked on the small gas grill. Once, she heard a high-pitched voice wail, "But I don't like eggs, and sausage is so *greasy!*" and had to restrain herself from shouting back, "Then don't eat, Nancy!" Throughout the leisurely meal and afterwards while helping wash up, she caught occasional glimpses of Tif, who seemed to be everywhere, directing, supervising, explaining. He examined the sky, the cliffs, the water, then gathered them all together.

"We want to leave this site as clean—or cleaner—than we found it," he stated firmly. "As you pack up your gear, I want all of you to check for stray litter. All flammable trash will be burned in the metal box. The ashes and all unburnable garbage will be carried out with us in sturdy canvas bags. Remember, we all own a piece of this land, so let's take care of it."

People scattered to begin packing and stowing gear, to oversee the burning of trash, to wash up. Andy started toward her bag, trying to remember just how Rick had shown her to roll it and the mat together when once again her arm was captured. At this rate, she thought with a sigh, her upper arm would be permanently bruised by the end of the trip. She turned to request release from bondage and discovered Tif scowling at her.

"I thought I told you to wait," he said.

"Karla and Nancy asked me to . . . help them out," she answered, hoping he wasn't the type to demand details.

"Next time when I say wait, you wait for me."

Well, here was the man Carol had described! But *she* was no doormat, to lie beneath his feet at his command. If he expected blind obedience from this female, thought Andra with flaring hostility, Tif Wilson was about to receive a jolt worthy of the roughest rapids!

"I might just do that," she said coldly, "when you say please."

She subconsciously braced her weight on her heels, preparing for his raging retort. She was nearly unbalanced when he merely crinkled his eyes at her, emphasizing their downward slant. Her lips parted, but no sounds came from between them. Andra couldn't think of a single thing to say.

While she stood staring at him, Tif pulled a fat tube out of a shirt pocket and began unwinding the cap. "You're going to burn to blisters unless you get more protection. Your face is already pink, and I doubt it's used to any sun."

That was true. Her skin was normally so fair as to appear translucent, and Andy had never been one to strive for a tan. She realized now why he'd been frowning at her earlier and felt utterly foolish.

"I'm afraid I never gave it a thought," she confessed with a half smile. "Is that lotion? Thanks."

She put out her hand for the tube, but he didn't give it to her. Instead, he squeezed the lotion onto his fingers, then tipped her head back and began to apply the sunscreen to her brow, nose, cheeks, chin. The circling rhythm of his touch was tranquilizing, yet disturbingly tingly. When he finished and withdrew his fingers, Andra had to swallow a sigh of regret. She'd been wishing he would go on and on touching her.

"There," he said with satisfaction. "That ought to help. But keep your hat on and your shirt buttoned. And keep the sleeves down. It'll be hot today, but we'll gradually roll them up at intervals so your arms can get used to the sun. With all the reflection off the water, the sun is deadly in the canyon. You need to be careful."

Before she could thank him, he was called away by someone else. She moved on to tussle with her personal gear and found Rick kneeling by her bag, about to roll it up.

"Let me do it," she insisted, running up beside him. "If I don't learn now, I'll never get it right. I can't keep having you do these things for me."

"Sounds like you've been listening to our fearless leader

again," teased Rick. But he leaned back, letting Andy take over and issuing occasional casual instructions. "It seems you were wrong—you two seem to be getting along well. *Quite* well." He threw a searching look at her which Andy chose to ignore. "I guess we panicked over nothing. After all, it's been over two years since his divorce, and lord knows we see enough divorces to know that people do get over it and adjust."

Andy paused. Except, perhaps, when love ran too deep. She didn't think Tif had gotten over his divorce. Maybe he'd decided she wasn't the wicked attorney he'd thought her, but he certainly harbored resentments over losing Carol. The notion nearly choked her. She realized Rick was watching her closely and managed a shrug. "Oh, some do and some don't."

"Well, I don't think we need to worry any longer about his tipping us into the river for revenge."

She finished tying her roll into a bundle. "No, I don't think we have to worry about that," she agreed, thinking of the look in his eyes, the draw of his breath when she'd pulled off the T-shirt. He'd keep her around, she thought cynically, if only for entertainment.

They lugged their gear down to the shore, where once again it was lashed into the rafts and covered with heavy tarps. In answer to Karla's beckoning wave, Andy and Rick moved to sit beside her in the shade. They passed the time exchanging light banter while watching great blue herons lift and flap downriver. Three scantily clad coeds from Wisconsin circled Tif, questioning him about the depth of the river, the height of the canyon walls, the speed of the current. Andra strove not to notice how often they broke into giggles over his low replies.

"What are we waiting for?" asked Nancy, the pitch of her voice shrilly demanding.

"For the water to rise," answered Tif, exhibiting a patience which surprised Andra. "The river is controlled by the engineers of the Glen Canyon Dam." He said it with a contempt seconded by each of the boatmen, and immediately the group fell into a lively discussion on the merits, or lack of them, of the dam.

By noon the water level was high enough for them to put in. Just before pushing off, Tif and the other oarsmen made a swift, last-minute search to make certain the campsite was left as they'd found it, soft sand strewn with nothing more than rocks and shrubs. Tugging on her lower lip with her teeth, Andra watched and tried to pretend she didn't care which raft she rode in today. Knowing that self-deceit was the worst lie of all, she gave it up as the men returned to the launch site and admitted to herself that if Tif didn't want her in the lead raft, she was going to be hurt. No matter how ridiculous it was, she knew it to be true.

When Tif gestured to her, Rick, Karla, and Brent, Andy's first reaction was relief. But as the raft slipped into the water, fright took over. She clenched the nylon grips until her long nails punctured her palms. She studied the differing browns on the stained leather gloves Tif wore, then watched the buckles of his open life jacket flap as he rowed. The sun glinted over the slick perspiration oiling his skin. The powerful flexure of muscles in his arms, shoulders, legs, somewhat reassured her. He wasn't the man to lose control of the raft. After a time he stopped rowing and they silently drifted.

The canyon filled with stillness. A sparrow hawk flew up from the thickets along the bank. Tif began speaking of the canyon, of the different theories of its formation. Listening to the steady flow of his pleasantly low voice, Andra relaxed totally. The straps lay loosely in the flat of her hand.

Why had she been so scared? This wasn't bad at all! The prismatic sparkle of the sun tripped lightly over the blue-green surface of the water. The variegated colors of limestone cliffs shone like rainbows. Directly above, clouds skimmed through blazing blue sky. All around them, canyon wrens warbled and the distant boom of thunder rumbled.

Thunder rumbled? Andra again glanced at the clear sky, then cast a questioning look at Rick.

"Soap Creek Rapids," he announced in the tone of a judge pronouncing sentence.

All her fear returned with a sickening crash. She nearly slapped Rick when he went on to inform her it had a rating of 8, heavy, and a fall of seventeen feet, but she was afraid to even momentarily loosen her grip on the gear straps to do it.

Deafened by an enormous roaring, Andra peered past Tif's shoulder and froze. The river simply dropped out of sight; the flat sheet of water disappeared into nothingness. Her view was mercifully blocked as Tif stood to check their position. He was rowing with the current, and abruptly the water accelerated, gripping the raft and sweeping it onward. Andy knew what to do. She shut her eyes and tightened her hold.

Exploding waves rushed at the raft, drenching them with shockingly cold water. Unwillingly, Andra's eyes popped open. What she saw terrified her beyond the ability to close them again. A sculpture of water towered at least twelve feet into the air, standing fixed as the small craft hurtled sideways toward it. Berylline waves leapt over them, punching the rocking raft and burying them in the icy water. Several fast, solid thuds convinced Andra they were drowning. Unbelievably, Tif's strong arms bent the oars, altering their course and sending them past rocks and holes of water into a calm stretch known as a pool.

Concentrating on breathing, Andy sat stunned, merely grateful to be alive. Tif glanced over his shoulder, then winked. Rick handed her a bucket, and she automatically began to help remove the Colorado River from the raft. As she recovered her senses, she turned on Rick.

"Don't you ever give me a rapids rating again! I don't want to know, do you understand?" she hissed. Tif heard and laughed, so she rounded on him. "And you! What was that damned thing back there?"

"Just a haystack—a standing wave. They're caused by the deceleration of the current." She looked blank, so he expanded. "When fast-moving water slams into slow water, it causes the waves to stand still, rising upward, not forward like ocean waves."

"Did you know about this?" she demanded of Rick. "First scorpions, now standing waves! Why didn't somebody *tell* me?"

She got no sympathy, only laughter from everyone in the boat, and Andy had sense enough to laugh along with them. As they continued downriver, they hit rapids every two or three miles until the undulating rush down the tongue of water, the quick jumping waves, the bailing buckets, almost became routine. Baptized again and again by the surging waves, they were alternately sodden by the freezing waters and baked dry by the heated sun. Andy never stopped being afraid, but her fear seemed to add to her excitement, making it intensely pleasurable. An acute, sensual thrill of achievement pulsed in her each time they came out of the roiling rapids into the pools.

By the time they put in on a beach above the North Canyon to make camp for the night, Andra felt she'd been on the river at least a lifetime. Her arms ached from gripping in terror and bailing in relief, and despite all her precautions, her nose, chin, and throat were tinged a bright shade of pink. As soon as they were unloaded, she felt she'd earned the right to rest and staggered off to unroll her bag. Even the hearty aroma of mulligan stew filling the camp air failed to tantalize. Andy wanted the benevolent blankness of sleep.

Tif, however, had other plans. He stopped her in mid-step, dumped her bag and duffel without looking where they fell, and began examining her tenderly burned skin.

"Tif, please, all I want is to take a nap," she wearily sighed.

"Not until we've done something about this. You think it stings now, wait a few hours." He dragged her along, her protests barely whispered, until they came to the watertight locker which held, among other things, the medical kit. He rummaged through this and came up with an ointment which he assured her would do the trick. At the moment she hadn't enough energy to care if it did or not.

As others moved busily around them, fixing dinner, setting up camp, playing on the beach, Tif began to spread the ointment into her skin. She sat passively in the sand as he did so; she offered no resistance when he pushed her gently back, toppling her prone. He undid her first two shirt buttons and rubbed the ointment down her throat, over the exposed, pinked skin of her breastbone. A strange energy seemed to race from his fingers into her blood, displacing her tired, drugged feeling.

Her eyelids had lazily drifted down; Andra peeped at him through her long, heavy lashes. He appeared to be concentrating on applying the ointment, but she noted a deepening of the color beneath his tan and a quickening of his breath. A tremor of eager response rippled through her. Her earlier rationalizations about not getting involved with this man vanished in the hypnotic spell of his cadenced touch. All too soon, that magical touch withdrew. Her eyes opened fully, and Tif pulled her to her feet.

"You may think you're not hungry, but you'll be glad to eat. Come help me dish out the stew."

"Must you always think you know what's best for me?" she asked in a voice thick with resentment. All she wanted was sleep!

"Always," he replied complacently. "Remember that, Andra. Here, I'll always know what's best for you."

"Humph! Sure you will," she muttered, but allowed him to steer her toward the fire.

Later she had to acknowledge that he *had* been right. The stew was marvelous, and she'd discovered she was ravenous. After eating, her spirit revived, and she happily did her share of the cleanup. Later she joined in watching in awed appreciation as colored layers of surrounding rock burst in a dazzling Fourth of July fireworks display. The cliffs shone ruby, then gilt, as the sun lowered its gold leaf rays over them. Darkening shadows emphasized the brilliance of the inspiring sunset. It moved Andra in an unexplainable emotional way, heightening her gratitude that Tif had not let her miss this.

The growing camaraderie of the group deepened when Mike, the oarsman with the droopy mustache and cheery grin, took out a handmade recorder and began to play. A hushed spirituality covered them all as haunting notes rose above the colossal cliffs to fade into the night air. Andy sat in a ball, knees drawn forward, chin resting against them. This sensuous contentment, this shared companionship after the day's dangers and hard work, felt almost erotic in its intensity. She luxuriated in the feelings washing through her, and when Tif tapped on her arm to draw her from the ring of listeners, she nearly stretched and purred at him.

It was another moonless night, which only served to stimulate Andra's mysterious excitement. She followed Tif wordlessly, knowing that his need for silence in this still night was as great as hers. He brought her to a sweep of sand beyond a slight ridge above the camp and they sat, cross-legged, not touching, listening to the faint cries of the recorder.

Just how long they sat so quietly, Andy had no way of knowing. It seemed a timeless eternity before he pressed her softly, softly into the sand, before he leaned his strong, shapely body next to hers, before he lightly twisted his fingers into her hair. Still he did not kiss her. He did not bring his lips to hers until Andra, bursting with an aching need, moaned, "Please."

The heated silence of his kiss muffled her entreaty. As naturally as rose petals unfurled to meet the sun, her lips unfolded to meet his again and again. Each kiss was a raindrop sprinkling her parched soul. She wanted to drown in a deluge of his kisses.

Tif slipped his rough-palmed hand beneath her shirt, slowly stroking the satiny skin of her midriff, deftly fanning the flames of her burning need. He inched his hand upward, exploring her with deliberation, leisurely drawing out their pleasure. It was exquisite torment.

With an abrupt, hungry groan, Andra arched eagerly toward his touch. Her blood pulsed with wanting, needing. She wanted to feel the hardness of his body against hers. She needed to feel his flesh fusing into hers.

Quivers of longing leapt from one to the other, and Tif's patience fell away. He curled his palms urgently, possessively over her breasts, rubbing restlessly over her extended nipples through the sheer fabric of her bra, then jerked his hands from under her shirt to fumble impatiently with the buttons. Murmuring an indistinct chant against her skin, he slid his lips feverishly down her jaw, over the tingling column of her sunburned throat.

Nuzzled within the shadows of the night, embraced by the softly shifting sand beneath her, enveloped by the solid length of him above her, Andra felt as if this were the single moment she had been existing for.

This had been in her subconscious all day, from the moment upon wakening when she'd answered the challenge in Tif's eyes. This was what she'd wanted; this was what she'd feared.

Perspiration thinly lacquered his skin and scented the

air with his maleness. Andra delighted in it, in everything. She savored the tautness of the thigh thrust against hers, the moist warmth of the tongue tickling her lips, the sandlike texture of the palms grazing over her skin. Spreading open his unbuttoned shirt, she splayed her fingers over the smooth sinews of his chest. The quickening thud of his heart beneath her fingertips excited her, and she hungrily ran her hands down the flat planes of his muscled stomach.

A distant voice did not at first disturb them. But after several moments it became clear that someone was calling for Tif. He lay very still over Andy, his lips nestled in the hollow of her neck. Only his unsteady, harsh breath sounded between them. "Damn," he quietly cursed in a thickened voice. He sighed, then kissed her once, lightly but firmly, and released her. As he stood, he said huskily, "Later. We'll finish this later."

Andra sat up with a jerk. Chills as iced as the river water dashed over the heated pulsing of her blood. What the hell had she been doing? Was she crazy? Their sudden, restless intimacy had dizzied her, but now she was all too clearheaded. He bent and held out a hand to help her up, but she ignored it, shaking her head. "No," she said, reinforcing her denial.

"What?" Tif dropped his hand and straightened. "What do you mean?"

"I mean," she explained on a slightly shaky breath as she scrambled to her feet, "that we won't finish this later."

"What?" he asked again in mounting irritation.

"This was just a crazy interlude. The—the sunset, the music, the whole day, just added up to *pow*. It didn't really mean anything."

"So what happened just now? Nothing?"

"Nothing of any substance. It was a—a moment in passing. Really, we should be grateful that you're wanted back at camp or things might have become terribly complicated."

"Complicated," he repeated, and Andy's throat constricted. His voice was cold, tight, laced with anger. The graded lines of his jaw locked into place, and he said through his teeth, "You're saying that if you had made love to me just now, it would have been a mere accident."

Andy winced. He made it sound like a cruel insult, something she'd never meant at all. "No, I—"

"Well, thank you very much, lady!" snapped Tif in throbbing tones. He spun around, calling out, "I'm coming, damn it, I'm coming!" He took several steps, stopped, and threw over his shoulder, "I'd almost begun to think you were human, which shows you how gullible I can be. I keep forgetting you career-driven women are automated bitches without anything so inconvenient as feelings to get in the way of success."

He was gone before Andra could gather her wits to respond to his last, unbelievable charge. She stood, wondering what she had done, why she had done it. *Why* had she turned him down? Sometimes she'd said yes, sometimes no, to such propositions in the past, but this was the first time she'd ever said no when she wanted to say yes.

Andra had wanted very much to say yes.

She wanted Tif; she couldn't remember ever feeling so aroused, so hungry for another soul in all her life as she had in those delirious minutes with him. So why had she been so definite about not carrying on later?

She wasn't very sure she really wanted to know the answers. Andra was all too afraid that the reply had nothing to do with her and everything to do with a petite TV program director named Carol. She didn't think she could bear being a substitute for Tif's ex-wife! Shying away from examining this too closely, she began to swipe the sand from her clothes and hair, then tucked her shirt neatly into her jeans and returned to camp.

CHAPTER FOUR

The last cry of the recorder faded into the sapphire sky, and the hushed murmur of voices fell to a low intimacy. Andra poised a moment, studying the travelers caught between sand and stars, feeling removed from the fellowship penetrating the small circle. She noted an unconscious pairing off beginning among them. The trio of college girls had separated, one leaning in the arms of a dentist from Louisiana and another sitting with an architect from California. The third was deep in conversation with the bearded boatman named Steve.

Her gaze casually swept the couples dotted over the beach and paused. Isolated from everyone else, Tif sat beside Karla, his silvery head bent close to her dark tresses. *That might have been me.* With an impatient click of her tongue, Andra turned away from such reflection. She should be damned glad it wasn't!

She slipped unobtrusively into place beside Rick. He glanced at her, grinned, and returned his attention to the two men with whom he'd been discussing the problem with the DH rule in baseball. Boredom settled over Andy. She tried not to notice the couples who snuggled together, laughed together, whispered together. She refused to notice one particular couple at all. Just as she decided to excuse herself and turn in for the night, a voice raised to ask Tif what was ahead in the morning. His answering chuckle held her in place.

Andra told herself she wouldn't look at him, but her eyes refused to listen. His arm lay casually draped over Karla's shoulders, his body pressed closely against hers. A mingling of anger and dejection took Andy by surprise. Surely, she couldn't be *jealous!* She had no reason! She hardly knew him, after all. And what she knew, she didn't even like!

"More river, more rapids, more sun and"— Tif drew a long breath—"more fun."

Everyone laughed. The mood swiftly changed to a comfortable congeniality. The circle seemed to constrict. People drew closer together. Andy felt like the odd man out.

"This is so . . . so *intense*," said a woman with short auburn curls. Andy thought her name was Penny. Her owl-shaped glasses reflected the wavering hues of the fire as she looked around at them all. "I've never felt so close to people so quickly in my life. I feel like, well, like I've known all of you all my life!" She ended with a self-conscious giggle and slid within the hold of her husband's arms.

Several voices agreed with her. Andra remained silent. Tif nodded. When he spoke, even the river seemed to strain to listen.

"It happens on every river trip. For two weeks this is your community, your family, all you have. The danger, the achievement, the isolation, the natural sensuality surrounding us—it all works to draw people together."

"I'll say," chimed in the dentist on a slow southern drawl. He tightened his clasp on the shapely young beauty at his side.

"Let's hear it for the river trip!" someone called out from the shadows, bringing another round of laughter.

"Settings like this are designed to bind people together, emotionally and physically," said Tif quietly. "The atmosphere is erotically sensuous. Your awareness of what's around you is intensified. The warmth of the sun, the slick chill of the water, the clash of sound against silence. It's only natural for you to reach out to share that with someone else, to experience the heightened sensitivity you feel with another soul, another body."

This time no one made suggestive jokes. They sat in a stillness almost reverent. Tif's words had been filled with a humble respect. It was clear that he loved this stretch of land, this length of river. He loved the companionship and the communion it wrung from people who might otherwise not exchange more than the time of day. For once, even Nancy Hartigan had nothing to say.

Shortly after, the camp dissolved into individual pockets of privacy. Andy spread out her mat and bag beside Rick's, then paused with Tif's gray T-shirt in her hand. He hadn't said a word to her since the incident on the ridge; when he'd looked at her at all, his eyes had skated coldly past her, like sharpened blades over ice. Under the circumstances she didn't think she should wear his T-shirt to sleep in. Shoving it back into her duffel, she pulled out the short cotton nightie she'd packed and tugged it half on while discarding her other clothes. When she lay down, she firmly ignored the flutter of hope that Tif would soon bring his bag to sleep beside her.

After a time she heard Rick crawl onto his bag. Eventually she heard his light snore. Tif did not come. She lay thinking about what he'd said tonight and realized that what she'd told him about everything just adding up to "pow" had been, for him, the simple truth. He'd told them all it happened every trip. It probably did. But what had happened to her would not happen on any other trip; she was certain of it. What had happened to her had been too special, too unique, to be blamed solely on the elements.

Obviously, however, for Tif it had been just another episode of heightened senses in the canyon. She envisioned him now with Karla, sharing the awareness. Were they making love? Were they twined together within his sleeping bag? The image left Andy feeling clammy. She hadn't experienced such gut-wrenching insecurities since she was in high school agonizing because Dick DeCelles took Sueanne Barton to the prom. Well, it was ridiculous to feel them now. She'd never had a chance with Tif anyway. His heart belonged to Carol.

The sand-bed that had been surprisingly comfortable the night before now seemed torturously hard and lumpy. After tossing and turning for several hours, she'd fallen into a mere doze to awaken at the first hint of dawn. No one else was stirring. Andy took advantage of the fact to rise and dress in solitude. She again donned the plain bone-white shirt and blue jeans she'd had on the day before. She rolled the sleeves to her elbows, then soundlessly brushed her teeth and hair, washed her face, and repacked. The quietude was awesome. A sense of tranquillity settled over her, and her restless discontent of the previous evening was forgotten.

Without thinking about spiders or other creatures, she yanked on her shoes and walked away from the camp. Lord, but Tif was right. Everything—the slate of the sky visible above the crooked canyon rim, the silent scampering of a lizard over a rock, the clinging caress of air already beginning to heat up, the constant gurgle and slap of the river—everything was more vivid, more impressive than she'd have thought possible. Andra felt more aware, more alive. About a mile from the camp she scaled several stones and sat near a prickly hedgehog cactus. In this shaded sanctum she let her mind meander into the dawn.

She thought about the years of struggle to finish near

the top of her class at law school. She thought about the years since, striving to establish herself as a top-notch attorney. She thought about how her circle of friends had diminished as she became more deeply involved in courts and clients and they in homes and families. She thought about the few men who'd meant anything to her and how they'd all somehow faded from her life over the years. Running like a binding thread through all her musings was the question, what was she to do with her life?

Every person controlled his own destiny. Andra firmly believed this. If you weren't happy with the progression of your life, then you should change it, not wait for it to change. Her problem was that she didn't know what changes should be made. The satisfaction from her career hadn't been as deep in the past months. Had she made a mistake? She didn't think so, not really, but she wasn't sure.

Drawing her knees up to her chin, Andy gazed up at the battlemented turrets of buff and cream and red rock looming above and wondered if she would find the answers here. Her body tensed as she listened. She heard no answers, but she certainly heard the question.

"What the hell are you doing?"

The ball of her body exploded. Her arms flew outward; the back of her hand struck the cactus. She jerked it back with a yelp, then glared accusingly at the glowering image of Tif Wilson. His gray eyes smoldered like smoke signals. The message wasn't pleasant.

She looked at her hand and gingerly extracted a cactus needle. "None of your business," she muttered.

Tif curled his long fingers painfully around her wrist and hauled her to her feet so rapidly she had no time to utter a protest. He shook her arm once, jarring Andy to her back teeth, then dropped it as if he found the merest touch of her distasteful.

"Who the hell do you think you are, *counselor*?" he

asked in a nasty tone. "Do you think it amusing to have an entire camp dancing to your whims?"

"But I only wanted—"

"This isn't your courtroom, lady, and what you want means little here!"

The low growl resembled the bellow of a steam whistle. Andra recognized it and shut her opened mouth on a snap. This was the unreasonable, uncivilized man she knew only too well! She didn't intend to even attempt to offer a rational explanation. The man didn't know what rational was. She again focused her attention on her throbbing hand.

"Just what kind of game were you playing?" he demanded. "Hide and seek?"

Her silence acted like the detonator on a charge of TNT. He grabbed her arm and wrenched her down the stones. Digging in her heels, Andy tried to skid to a stop. With one hard shake he towed her onward. Her adrenaline was pumping furiously, and she put every ounce of strength she possessed into regaining her arm. When she managed to pull free of his clasp, it was so unexpected she stumbled and sprawled headfirst into the sand.

Maybe she ought to reconsider giving him an explanation. "I didn't mean—" she began while sputtering sand from her lips.

"Didn't you?" he cut in on a sneer. "You didn't mean to have the entire camp searching for you for the past forty minutes? Then why didn't you tell someone where you were going?"

Andra stared up the length of him, past the tanned legs, frayed cutoffs, beautifully bared chest, and directly into the face stained with rage. She tried, she really tried, to say something to placate him, but she'd lost her voice.

"How the hell were we to know you hadn't taken it into your head to try swimming in the river?" continued Tif savagely. Without the least pretense of kindness, he bent and plucked Andy to her feet. "I'm going to tell you this just once, so listen up. From now on, you don't go as far as the toilet without telling someone what you're doing."

He spun and began stalking away. In a daze Andy sprinted after him. She touched his arm. He stopped but didn't look at her. She cleared her throat, then cleared it again. When she found her voice at last, it had rusted.

"I'm sorry. I didn't realize . . ."

"Just don't forget I mean what I say. Don't ever wander off alone again." He strode away, leaving Andy covered with sand and humiliation.

She heard him call out, telling them he'd found her, and she longed for an invisibility shield. She walked into the campsite feeling like a dog with her tail between her legs. Some eyed her with hostility, some with compassion. Others ignored her. When Rick approached her with a smile on his lips and concern in his eyes, she nearly threw herself on him in relief.

"You ready for some breakfast, doll?" he inquired, dropping his arm over her shoulder.

"I—no, I'm not really hungry. I'll just go get my hat and life jacket on." She was positive even the tiniest bite of food would make her gag. Her stomach was churning like a high-speed blender out of control. She took a step, then jumped as someone touched her shoulder.

"Sorry, didn't mean to shock you," said Karla in her friendly way. She held up a pair of tweezers and some ointment. "Tif said you'd fallen in some cactus, and I've come to play nurse."

Andra looked at her hand and was surprised to remember that it hurt. She'd forgotten the ache in the argument with Tif. Now, however, darts of pain pricked at her. She raised her dulled eyes to the clear blue sympathy in Karla's. "Yes," she said flatly. "It hurts."

"Rick, why don't you go get us some plates of breakfast while I take care of Andy's hand?" Karla drew Andy down to sit cross-legged on the sand while she attentively withdrew cactus needles with her tweezers. "What a mess! Well, be thankful it's the back of your hand that got kissed by the cactus and not your palm."

"Why?"

"Think how painful gripping the gear straps would be!" replied Karla with a laugh. She dabbed ointment on and said in a motherly way, "We'll have to wait until the deeper ones come back to the surface to dig them out." She gave Andy back her hand, then patted her shoulder gently. "Don't worry about it. Before the day is out, everyone will be laughing over this morning's hunt. Worse mistakes can happen—and probably will before we reach the end of the trip."

Andra tried to smile, but her mouth was stiff. Her whole body felt stiff. When Rick arrived with the tin plates heaped with food, her hands, arms, lips, couldn't seem to work together. She dropped a forkful of egg in her lap, then spilled coffee over her sore hand. After a halfhearted attempt to enjoy the bite that finally did make it to her mouth, Andy gave up. She wasn't hungry. She was too depressed to bother with food.

It wasn't that she'd inconvenienced the camp, though she was sincerely sorry for that. It wasn't even the pain of her hand. The leaden weight in her soul stemmed solely from Tif Wilson's contemptuous dismissal. How was she going to get through the next twelve days?

A stridulous whine pierced the buzz and hum of activity. "But it's positively primitive!" screeched Nancy. "And there were *tracks* beside my bed this morning. *Things* have been crawling over me all night!"

Andy glanced toward Nancy in time to see Tif bestow one of his kindest smiles on the blonde. "That's not likely," he said in tones to match his smile. "The creatures of the canyon are far more afraid of us than we are of them."

Other sounds rose as their voices dropped, drowning

out the conversation. But Andy had heard enough to perceive Tif's patience with the ever-complaining Nancy. Why, she thought with rising hostility, doesn't he ever yell at *her?* She felt unjustly abused and took a small measure of delight in picturing Wilson saddled with Nancy's wailing laments for the whole of the trip. She couldn't think of anyone who deserved it more.

She went with Karla to help clean up and pack the dishes. It seemed Karla had been right; already, she was the subject of teasing innuendoes regarding her matutinal disappearance. Mike stroked his mustache and fixed a leering grin on her, then drawled suggestively, "If you're into cacti, I could arrange a hot date with an ocotillo I know."

In the general laughter Andy's inner wounds began to heal. Following Mike's lengthy lecture on the proper manner in which to caress a hostile cactus into submission, she was feeling more like her usual sensible self, able to view the morning with a clearer perspective. What had happened, after all? Tif had understandably lost his temper with her. He was responsible for the entire group, and he had every right to be angry over her stupid misjudgment. She'd apologize to him as soon as she could.

Pleased with her resolution, certain that everything would soon be set right, Andra hummed happily as she slapped shut the silver ammo can in which bread and eggs were stored. One of her fingernails caught on the edge of the lid and ripped. She examined it in dismay. The deep cinnamon polish on all her nails had already chipped and cracked, giving her hands the appearance of a drudge's, but this was irreparable. The nail was split almost to the tip of her finger.

"Oh, no!" she groaned. She licked her index finger, then nibbled the broken nail off. Looking at the short, ragged remainder, she swore loudly. "Drat and damn!"

"Something wrong?" inquired a voice that held no sympathy.

She whirled on Tif, still frowning. "I broke my nail on that damn can," she said petulantly.

"What's one less claw to you? You've still got more than enough to scratch with," he returned with a tight disdain that drained the color from Andra's face.

She stood as motionless as the rock surrounding her. To think she'd intended to apologize to this... this *creep!* He had plenty of patience, sympathy, and goodwill for everyone else on this trip, but not for her. Oh, no, not for the woman who had helped his wife get free of him. She'd been right from the first. He resented her, and he meant to make this the most rotten experience of her life. The fact that he was succeeding beyond the wildest expectations only made her more determined than ever to never let him know how miserable she was feeling. Andy tipped her chin up and directed a pointed glare at him.

"If you'll excuse me, Mr. Wilson, I have a river trip to finish." She pushed past him and didn't look back. She had one wish: to get through this damned canyon and then never set eyes on Tif Wilson again. She couldn't imagine how she'd thought even briefly that he meant anything to her. Generally, the kind of man he was left her cold. *He* left her cold!

When they got ready to launch, Andy held back, refusing to get into the lead raft, and was grateful when Rick stayed with her. Together, they got into the third boat with the oarsman who had the long brown hair and gold earring. His name, she later learned, was Dennis.

Being behind other rafts was, Andy quickly decided, much worse than being in the lead. She now had unwanted previews of what was coming, for as they approached each new rapid, she saw the rafts ahead disappear, then occasionally dance back into sight before vanishing altogether in the roiling waters. She reminded herself that back home she'd actually twice ridden the Screamroller with its loop-the-loops. Surely that counted for something.

The canyon, which seemed ever the same, was constantly changing. A slope above the river came into view, bringing astonished gasps from everyone. It was covered in greenery that appeared lush compared to the sparse vegetation preceding it. Red, yellow, and orange wildflowers shone like gems set against rocks of gold and rust. Water sprayed down the cliffs, glittering like cut crystal in the sunlight. As they pulled ashore for a drink of clear spring water, Dennis explained that this was Vasey's Paradise.

It seemed aptly named for everyone except Andy. While a water fight broke out with much laughter among the coeds and their friends, she hovered restively, anxious to move on, to reach the end of the journey. Rick took several photos of the action, then abruptly aimed his camera at Andra. She obediently cracked her lips in a facsimile of a smile, but it quickly faded at the sight of Tif and Karla sitting together.

A mile downriver they again pulled in, this time to lunch at Redwall Cavern. The gingered limestone curved like a gigantic bandshell, and they sat on smooth, white sand in the shade of its vaulted ceiling. Andy nibbled with disinterest on a sandwich and drank half a glass of lemonade. She was too listless to protest when Rick suggested she pose for a few pictures within the cavern. She imagined herself back home, looking at these photos and saying, "So that's what it looked like!" because she certainly wasn't seeing much of the sights now. Every time she looked around, her eyes riveted on layers of hair nearly as bleached as the sand, and it would take all her control to focus blindly on something else.

Back on the river, Andy noticed that the color of the water had changed to a red-brown. The current, too, was much faster. Swirls of foam lazed down the river, then capered wildly as waves rushed and tumbled over one another to spatter against the raft. As the afternoon went on, her mind began to whirl like the waves, cavorting aimlessly, shying from memories of the night before and unable to settle on anything else. Early in the evening they made their third camp amidst several small redbud trees. Andy climbed out of the raft feeling warm and dizzy and uncaring whether she ate or not.

This experience was turning out to be as awful as she'd known it would be. Worse. She wished wholeheartedly that she had not come. Her head ached and wouldn't quit spinning. The protective ointment had long since worn off her hand, and it stung incessantly. Her nose, chin, and neck prickled unpleasantly, and she didn't think she possessed a muscle that hadn't been overworked. As she waited with everyone else for the gear to be unpacked, she vowed that when she got back to Kansas City—*if* she got back to Kansas City—she'd never go near so much as a *tub* of water.

Setting up camp had by now become routine. Carrying her duffel and sleeping roll, Andy staggered behind Rick to find a secluded spot to bed down. Fumbling, she managed to shrug out of her bulky life jacket and drop it carelessly on the ground. Rather than joining the crowd milling around the cookstove, she spread out her bag and stretched out. Just a nap, she told herself.

She thought at first she was still in the raft, rocking with the continuous motion of the water. When she dimly realized she was on the ground, she decided to ignore the vigorous shaking she was receiving. Her attempt to play possum failed as she was hefted upright and her cheeks each given a light, ringing tap. Her eyes flew open to gaze into unsmiling pewter-gray.

"Are you all right?" inquired a feminine voice.

Andra blinked, then lifted her eyes from Tif's to see Karla standing behind him, her pert features covered with anxiety. "Yes," she croaked in a dry voice. She glanced at

Tif's set face, then hurriedly shifted her attention back to the brunette. "I was just taking a nap."

She nervously licked her lips. Her forearms were still clasped within Tif's strong hands, and she was uncomfortably aware of the heat emanating from his palms. She was certain he was very angry with her and didn't think she had the strength to carry on her side of the argument. She swallowed what little saliva she had. "I'm sorry. I didn't mean to shirk my bit of the setting up. I'll clean up dinner."

Her struggle to rise was stymied by the fact that Tif hadn't released her. With the slightest of pressure, he held her firmly in place. "Karla, please bring Andy's dinner," he ordered.

As Karla spun away to do his bidding, panic seized Andra. She was feeling much too light-headed to deal with Tif's temper. She parted her lips to beg Karla to stay, but a mere squeak came out as his fingertips grazed her throat, then swept upward to her cheeks. She eyed him warily as he gently loosened the chin strap of her hat, then removed it to toss it into the sand. The breeze which blew over her head felt refreshingly cool. She felt giddy. Tif ruffled the sweat-matted locks of her hair.

"What's the matter with you?" he asked. For a change his question held no antagonism. His tone was so soft, Andra felt woozier than ever.

"N-nothing," she stammered. Why was she feeling so dizzy?

"Did you drink enough water today? Rick tells me you've hardly eaten a thing."

She tried a nod, but it left her faint. "Yes. I had some lemonade. And water at Eden."

He chuckled. "Paradise, but you've got the right idea." His eyes searched her face intently. "You're sure?"

"Ummm," was all she could manage beneath the force of his gaze. It occurred to her that it might be safer for her to have Tif angry. This gentleness of his would be her undoing.

He tipped her head back and examined her face, throat, breastbone, thoroughly. "The sunburn looks better, but after you eat, we'll spread more lotion on you to make sure. You have very tender skin, did you know that?" He wiggled the lobe of her ear, then stroked her jawline with his thumb. "You're not taking proper care of yourself, Ms. James. If you don't start, I'll have to take over. Would you want that?"

His voice had dropped to a husky rasp that raised bumps on Andy's skin. She had an irresistible urge to answer, "Yes, I would, very much," but was saved from this folly by the return of Karla with both Rick and a plate of barbecued chicken in tow.

Tif straightened away from her to take a can of beer from Rick, and Andra knew a strange sense of loss. As she accepted the plate and mug of water from Karla, she wished she could dislike the brunette, but there wasn't a remote possibility of it. Karla was just too damn likable. Unfortunately, Tif clearly thought so, too.

Impatiently pulling on a few sparse strands of his dark hair, Rick sat on his haunches beside her. "Are you okay, kid?"

"Of course," she said with false brightness.

"Don't lie to me, now. Remember, I'm the one who can shred a lying witness with my whiplash tongue."

"I'm not, Rick, really," she lied. She not only felt dizzy, she had the sinking notion she felt sorry for herself. Sorry because Tif very naturally preferred pert and breezy Karla to her acid-tongued self. "I'm fine."

"Why don't you go away and let the lady eat her meal in peace?" suggested Tif. He said it jokingly, but the look accompanying it was stern enough to propel Rick to his feet.

"Aye, aye, sir," said Rick with a mocking salute.

"Come on, Karla, before Cap'n Bligh throws us in the brig."

"Don't you mean makes us walk the plank?" queried Karla with a saucy laugh.

"Oh, but that would be a terrible waste of a beautiful body," countered Rick. He quirked his brows and ran his gaze over Karla's curves, then added, "They don't make 'em like mine anymore."

Their receding laughter floated back, emphasizing the lingering silence between the two still seated on the ground. Muffled sounds of activity drifted up from the main camp below. The aroma of the barbecued meat wisped over her with every breeze. Andy stared down at the chicken, wondering what to do with it. She had never felt less like eating in her life. Why hadn't Tif gone with Karla and Rick? Was he waiting to pick a fight with her?

"Eat. You need it," said Tif slowly.

She raised her eyes to meet his. How could Carol have said he had eyes that pierced like lead arrows? How could she ever have thought them cold? They were warm, the gray of them settling over Andy now like a steamy mist. Disconcerted by her thoughts, she quickly looked down at her plate.

A fingertip skimmed over her cheek. "You would please me if you ate something, Andra."

That quiet request was more effective than a blistering command. Andy found herself chewing and swallowing, all without tasting, all to please him. When she'd eaten most of the meat and a portion of the salad, Tif took the plate and utensils from her hands and pressed the tin mug into her clasp.

"I owe you an apology," he said when she'd taken a sip.

She choked, spit water into the sand, and stared at him with wide, glittering, disbelieving brown eyes.

With a self-mocking smile, he turned away from her to gaze out over the beach. "I'm sorry about what I said last night. And today. I knew you didn't disappear this morning on purpose. But last night I thought you were being a tease. I was still so furious, all I wanted to do was lash out at you."

He glanced at her once, then away again. Andy thought her heart might just vault out of her chest. She set down the mug with a shaking hand and tried to catch a stray breath.

"All day I kept thinking about you, and it eventually dawned on me that you've only seen me at my worst. And perhaps heard things—exaggerated or distorted—from Carol. When I'd thought it through, I couldn't really blame you for being reluctant to have anything to do with me."

Her head was swimming. She pressed her palms against her temples. These weren't the things she'd expected him to say to her. "But it's not . . . well, maybe it is, but . . ." she foundered into an awkward silence.

His laughter bore the precise timbre of the water rushing over the rocks at Vasey's Paradise. He curled his hands over hers and drew them downward. "Can this truly be the stiff-lipped attorney I remember so vividly?"

"Stiff-lipped!"

"Stiff-lipped," he reaffirmed. He pushed her gently backward until she found herself prone against the sleeping bag, his solid weight beside her. He lazily tinkered with the middle button of her shirt, pushing it in and out and back into the slot between her rapidly heaving breasts. "And frozen. I was convinced you were inhuman, nothing but a robot. Then there you were at Lee's Ferry, looking nothing at all like the ultimate professional I remembered."

"How . . . ?" was all she could manage.

"Oh, rather like you do now, as a matter of fact. Unsure, mussed, womanly. You should come out of your courtroom more often, Ms. James. You're much more . . . interesting . . . as a woman."

The feathery caress of his breath as he leaned over her tantalized beyond measure. She tried to recall how little this meant to him, how he said it happened every trip, but her mind was too busy responding to her wildly leaping nerves. The feel of his flesh filled her fingertips as they splayed against his chest. The musky scent of his skin filled her nostrils as his neck pressed against her cheek. The heat of his molten gaze filled her eyes as he drew back to stare at her.

"I missed you today," he whispered hoarsely. "All day."

"You didn't appear to lack company," she pointed out breathlessly.

"Oh, but I lacked the company that counted most." Tif dropped a light kiss on her nose, then he pulled away from her altogether. Disappointed, Andy started to reach out for him, then froze. She could not take in so much as a single breath. His whole face compressed with stark desire as his gaze flickered from her brow to her mouth, down to her breasts and back up to her mouth. Her body burned wherever his gaze touched. Her lips ached to again know the taste of his. She watched wordlessly as, with a visible effort, he hauled himself to his feet, then stood looking down at her.

"I'm not going to rush you, Andra," he whispered in a husky rustle. "I want you to get to know the man I really am before you decide whether you might want me."

Before she could say a word, he scooped up the plate and mug and strode off into the gathering darkness. Andy was left reeling in the giddy throes of a mind-spinning vertigo.

CHAPTER FIVE

His touch was soothing and very, very cool. Andra's eyes fluttered open. Shadow laced with moonlight over sand and shrub as Tif squatted beside her.

In the darkness she saw the even gleam of his teeth as he smiled, the bright luster of his hair as his head bent toward her. Beyond his shoulder the darkened outline of steep cliffs stood as sentinels around them, seeming to separate them from the reality of time, place, people. The distant roll of the river lulled against the hushed stillness. A soft, warm wind rippled over her skin, carrying the sharp tang of the lotion as he spread it over her burned skin. Was she dreaming?

"Go back to sleep," ordered Tif as if in answer to her unspoken question.

His fingers swirled over her throat. She knew he could feel the acceleration of her pulse. "What . . . are you . . . doing?" she asked on a thread of sound.

"I'm trying to protect your lovely skin," he replied without pausing in his rhythmic massage. "Just relax and enjoy it."

She was enjoying it, very much, but she had no intentions of going back to sleep. Not that she would have been able to, pulsing as she was to the thrill of his touch. She wanted to watch the moonbeams weave silver into his hair; she wanted to feel the magic of his skin caressing hers; she wanted to inhale the breath which he expelled over her. It was madness, she knew that, but it was undeniably, excruciatingly rapturous madness.

He dabbed lotion on her cheeks, rubbing it into her skin in a circular motion. The tip of his finger brushed her lower lip. His hands stilled. Her heart stopped. Within a fraction of time he continued the mesmerizing motion over her face, and Andy's heart began knocking in wary excitement.

They were alone, utterly alone. She could see nothing but the rock, the brush, and the disturbing presence of Tif. She could hear nothing but the river, the wind, and the thud of her heart. It beat so loudly she was certain it rang in his ears as well as hers. She tried to cover it with a trembling query. "Where is everyone? What time is it?"

She felt his amusement in the vibration of his fingers, then heard it in his suggestive drawl. "It's past midnight and everyone is sleeping . . . or at least passing the time lying down."

"What are you doing here?" she croaked nervously. She had to ignore his provocative hints. She had to divert them both from the intoxication of this moonlit interlude.

"I told you, taking care of you."

"No . . ." Andra wet her lips with her tongue. She saw his eyes flick to her mouth and forced herself to speak. "No, I meant, what are you doing as a boatman? How . . . did you start doing . . . this?"

"Wouldn't you rather hear what I'd like to be doing now?" He chuckled at her sharp intake of breath and leaned back on his haunches to swipe excess lotion off his hands onto his cutoffs.

He'd thought of her all day, he'd said. He wouldn't rush

her, he'd said. But Andy stared at the lithe movement of his shadowed profile and felt incredibly rushed. She was dizzy with it. How had this happened so swiftly?

Just when she thought he wasn't going to answer her question, he began reciting, "I took my first raft trip about five years ago. Carol and I weren't getting along well. She always hated having me hang around all summer. I interrupted her routine. She said she needed to sort things out and suggested we take separate vacations."

His voice was empty. Andy wished she hadn't brought the subject up. "It doesn't matter," she put in quickly. "You don't have to tell me—"

"It's nothing I can't tell you, Andy. I'd like to think we have a lot to share."

She couldn't swallow for several seconds. He may still love Carol, but there was no doubt that he wanted her. His desire was clear. It was in the susurration of his voice, the tension of his body, the smoldering of his gaze. She understood his intentions completely, but her own reactions, her own inclinations, utterly confused her.

"Anyway, I came on a week-long trip with another teacher," he continued evenly. "We rode in a massive group on the baloney boats."

"Baloney boats?"

"The motorized pontoons that flash through the river without really taking the time to appreciate it. But even zipping down the canyon, even protected from most of the fury of the river, I knew I was hooked. I loved every moment of it."

He sat silently for a time. She saw the opaque silhouette of his hand as he casually sifted the sand. She shook with abrupt yearning, yearning to hold him, to ease away his hurt, to share his joy. "And then?" she finally prompted.

"Then I spent the next twelve months trying to convince Carol to go with me. She wouldn't. She hated the outdoors and refused to try rafting for me."

"I can understand that," said Andra flatly. "I'm afraid of all this, too."

"But you came."

"Yes, but it was only an impulse. I refused at first. Vehemently."

Tif shifted his weight. She could feel his bare thigh rub against her denims. Even through the cloth her nerve-endings jangled along her hip.

"Was it an impulse to please Rick?" inquired Tif tonelessly.

"No."

"Then what?"

A wide, sleepy yawn overcame her. She was glad for the excuse to sit up. She pulled her knees up to her chin and replied slowly, "I'm not sure I can explain. I guess I thought I might be able to sort out my life if I got completely away from it."

"Are you unhappy? I thought you liked being an attorney."

There was a certain inevitable harshness in his voice. Hearing it, Andy shrugged. "I do. Or I did. It's what I always wanted. I used to watch *Perry Mason* as a kid and fantasize that I was Raymond Burr, stunning the court with my pronouncements of guilt and innocence. When my friends were planning their engagements, their weddings, their families, I was planning for law school, for bar exams, for cases. I've been satisfied . . ."

"But . . .?" he probed, leaning close enough for her to feel the heat of his arm.

"But lately not so much," she supplied after a lengthy silence. "Rick asked me to come on this trip. At first, I told him no, definitely not. I'm not really the adventurous type. Up to now my idea of roughing it has been to go without power in a thunderstorm. Then one day, after spending all day in court wrangling over the settlement in my client's divorce—"

Andra snapped into speechlessness. How could she have been so stupidly tactless? Her tongue weighted with lead, and her body stiffened as she waited for him to say something snide. He said nothing.

She counted several thumps of her heart, then cleared her throat, forced her tongue to move and her lips to part. "Well, I thought, Is this what I've trained so hard to do? Wills and divorces and petty small claims? Contracts and paperwork? I realized I wasn't Perry Mason. Even Della Street handled more exciting stuff. I felt confused, dissatisfied. So I told Rick I'd go with him and . . . well, here I am."

"Is that why you wandered off yesterday, to be alone to sort things out?"

She felt as if she'd used up her quota of breath, so she simply nodded her head. Once again she received a jolt from this unexpectedly complex man.

"I know I was harsh with you. It was a combination of anger and fright," he confessed quietly. "You're so green—I was worried, really worried you'd gotten hurt somehow. You'll remember your promise not to wander off like that again, won't you?"

As she recalled, she hadn't promised, he'd ordered, but Andy meekly agreed. He rewarded her by saying huskily, "You won't need to, anyway. We'll solve your problems together."

Her heart tripped, then began to pound fiercely. "I—uh —you never finished telling how you became a boatman."

"Trying to change the subject again?" His pale straight brows rose in the shadows, and Andy melted in the warmth of his teasing.

"Yes," she admitted bluntly, half-smiling.

He looked away, staring into the opacity of the canyon night. "The second summer, I came back and took a trip like this, only in a wooden dory. The next summer, I got hired on as a crew member and really began to learn about the Colorado. Since the divorce, I've spent every summer doing this. It's both a testing and a cleansing of the soul."

She watched his hand idly toy with her discarded hat. Again, that extraordinary longing to protect him swept through her. As if he needed protection! She would do better to watch out for herself, and she knew it. Calling upon her courtroom voice, she coolly inquired, "Where's Rick?"

Her hat crumpled soundlessly into the sand. "I thought you had no aspirations in that direction," said Tif harshly. When she didn't respond, he went on more evenly, "He was with Karla the last time I saw him. I told him I'd look out for you."

There was nothing she could say, so she sat gazing at the celestial crescent brightly decorating the sky. Tif slid closer to her, and her nerves jumped.

"How's your hand?"

"Okay. It hardly stings at all."

As if he didn't believe her, Tif took hold of her hand and squinted against the darkness to examine it. "Still, I'll rub some ointment on it."

Moonlight poured over his blond hair like thick, rich cream. Andy was glad he held her hand, for otherwise she would have spread her fingers into the soft strands held so temptingly close. She imagined the feel of his hair brushing against her skin and shivered with desire. He glanced up before she could remove her gaze. Unveiled hunger surged from gray eyes to brown. Time halted and neither could look away.

"In the morning," he said unsteadily. He released her hand and brought his hands to her shoulders. "For now . . . there are more important things to do . . ."

He pressed her back, falling gently against her as he did so. The thundering of his heart sounded over the wild pounding of her own. She welcomed the clamor. It muted the inner objections she didn't want to hear. Nor did she want to see the rigid need on Tif's face. She closed her eyes and gave herself up to the pure excitement of her feelings.

She felt his breath mist her eyelids and his hands circle her throat. She felt his thumbs stroke her jawline and his lips nuzzle her cheeks. She felt the heat of his body blanket hers and the tension of his muscles straining with desire. Andra felt her own need expand until it filled every cell, every pore of her body.

As his lips passionately sought the secrets of hers, Andra wove her fingers through the abundant downiness of his hair and drew him closer, closer, as if she might draw him into her. She had never before been caught in such a vortex of desire, whirling with unrestrained delirium. She spun out of control as his hands slid over her from shoulder to breast to thigh and back in eager, ardent strokes. She wanted to cry out, to beg him to touch her again and again, never stop, but his mouth still held hers in impassioned possession.

He didn't speak and she was glad. Words were unnecessary. He spoke instead with the fervor of his hands and lips, with the pressure of his hips against hers, with the warm sheen rising over his skin. The palms of his hands circled over her breasts and her nipples tautened, protesting against the barrier of her clothes. He abruptly pulled away, raising himself slightly to yank at the buttons on her shirt. Without the drug of his lips to cloud her senses, without the feverish skimming of his hands to rouse her body, Andy's mind took control with a loud demand to know what she was doing.

Opening her eyes unwillingly, Andra saw the stars, the moon, the majestic tiers of canyon rock. She saw Tif bend his head to place his lips against the swell of her breast. She saw his hands tug impatiently at the clasp of her bra. She knew he didn't love her. She didn't expect that, nor even really want it. But suddenly she couldn't bear to believe that it wasn't Andra James that brought this consuming need to him, that it was simply a powerfully erotic combination of elements. The sky, the river, the rock, the sand—these composed the setting designed, as Tif had said, to bring people together. She couldn't help wondering if he would have wanted her this way back in Kansas City.

Her flesh tingled as the cooling night air caressed it. She shivered, and Tif slid forward to again embrace her. Reaching up, Andy held him off. Pure physical sensation might be fine for others, but she needed emotional foundation for such a relationship. She needed to be desired for herself, not simply as a convenient body to experience the raptures of the great outdoors with. She saw his pale brows come together and wordlessly shook her head.

"What's wrong?" he whispered hoarsely.

Again she shook her head. But his instant scowl brought quivering words to her lips. "It's too soon. I'm . . . not ready for . . . this."

She didn't think he understood. He lay on his side, pressed against her, his hands held a breath away from her body. Then a slow, reluctant curve touched his lips. "Looks certainly can be deceiving. You seemed ready enough to me."

There was teasing laughter in his voice and a strong thread of regret that made Andy long to take back her words. But Tif was already lifting away from her. In a single fluid motion, he brushed her lips with his and rose to his feet. "Where . . .?" she started to ask, but he began spreading out his bag just inches away. When he had thrown off shirt and shoes, he lay down. Andy snuggled into her own bag, feeling more content. If he'd felt lust alone, he would never have accepted her refusal so readily.

Her serenity was shattered as he rolled toward her. He cupped her head between his palms and stared at her so fixedly she couldn't breathe.

"Just don't take too long to be ready for me," he muttered. He sprinkled several light, random kisses over her face, then added on a ragged note, "We don't have time to waste. The end of the river will come sooner than you think."

Each word stabbed at her. Each reinforced what she'd already suspected. The attraction he felt was spurred by the situation they were in. The attraction she felt was far more confusing. The desires she'd experienced with him far surpassed any she'd ever before known. She couldn't believe that such intense physical responses could be inspired solely by the setting. Yet, he wasn't really the type of man she usually felt drawn to. . . .

When Tif settled onto his bag with his back toward her, Andy shut her eyes, fighting the incredible urge to wreath her arms around him and tell him she was ready. She willed herself to sleep, but it was a restless sleep, a tossed and churning state filled with hot, disturbing images of herself entwined with the strong body so close beside her. It was a relief to be touched by morning light.

Thankful for the dawn, she sat up quickly. Her head whirled, and a shudder rippled down her body. She managed to stifle her low moan and pressing her palms against her temples, steadied herself enough to stand. Glancing at Tif's inert body, she silently pulled off her sleep-rumpled clothes and drew on a clean pair of jeans and a lemon terry cloth top. Every action seemed to take an unusual amount of effort, and Andy could only hope she wasn't getting sick. Even as she thought it, she feared she knew what was wrong with her.

She feared she had a bad case of Tif Wilson.

Once she was dressed, she sat back down on her bag and waited. Facing away from the distraction of the alluring male body asleep just inches away from her knee, Andy watched the sunlight meander over the castled cliffs and into the campsite. Odd tracks were highlighted in the sand, squiggles and dots which punctuated the earth and caused her to curl more securely on the safety of her bag. A scarcely audible rustling disturbed the serene silence. Heart accelerating, Andy looked over her shoulder to see a magnificent buck poised among the brush, pronged antlers quivering and huge, dark eyes warily watching her. In an instant the animal had disappeared, and she sighed her disappointment.

"Are you sighing because you've missed me?" asked Tif.

Wheeling with a force that left her dizzy, Andy faced him. He was sitting up, watching her. She hadn't heard him stir, and that annoyed her.

"Where did you learn to do that?" she inquired on a peevish note. "The Boy Scouts?"

He smiled, giving emphasis to his square lips and reminding Andy of the pliant warmth of them. It was precisely the sort of memory she'd wrestled with all night, and she had no wish to continue doing so. She frowned at him, and his smile seemed to harden.

"Do what?" he demanded.

"Sneak up on people," she replied unreasonably.

To her surprise the taut set of his mouth vanished. He grinned. "Do you always wake up this grouchy?" he asked with interest. He leaned forward and traced the full curve of her lower lip with his fingertip. "Or are you feeling unfulfilled?"

She angrily pushed his hand aside and stood up. "Neither. I'm just tired of waiting for you to wake up. And don't look so knowing! I didn't want to have you yelling at me if I'd gone to the bathroom before you woke up."

His soft laughter followed her as she pivoted and strode off in search of the toilet. She hadn't seen where it had been set up last night, but the ladies' was always upstream, the men's always downstream, so Andy followed the edge of the river until she located it tucked behind several small redbud trees. She leaned against a tree and watched dragonflies buzz by.

She hadn't actually felt any urge, other than the urge to be away from Tif. He disturbed her in more ways than she could count. Worst of all was this light-headed inability to think. She sucked in her lower lip and played her tongue over it. She wanted him; that much was clear. Her body responded to his like an instrument in the hands of a master musician. So why did she hold back? What made her say no when her body cried out its need?

Blowing out a long stream of air, Andra answered herself with one word. Carol. Tif's love for Carol certainly colored any feeling he might have for her. She suspected his initial attraction to her stemmed from a desire to get back at her for her part in his divorce. She further believed that Tif used the river trips—and the succession of women he no doubt had on them—as a means to purge his soul of his need for Carol. What Andy had to decide, if her head would only stop spinning long enough for her to do so, was whether or not Tif's motives mattered to her. Could she forget about Carol, about trips before and trips to come and simply enjoy Tif for the remainder of *this* trip?

Sounds of someone approaching broke into her reverie. Not that she'd been getting anywhere, anyway. Andy greeted Penny Jacobson and made her way back to her bedroll. At least she'd managed to make a decision. She'd decided not to make any decisions yet.

Tif was waiting for her. He stood watching her advance, arms akimbo, silhouetted by sunlight which bronzed his tawny skin. The ends of his unbuttoned cotton shirt hung beyond his cutoffs, and his hair was flattened on one side. To Andy's eyes he looked charmingly disheveled. And excessively appealing. Her step slowed, then stopped. In two sure strides he reached her. He pulled her into his arms, kissed her neck, and tickled her ear.

"You took your time," he said with a husky laugh that said much more. "I suppose you did it on purpose, just to torment me. I'll teach you soon enough that it doesn't pay to tease me. Now get packed up and come to breakfast."

He twirled her around, patted her bottom, and was gone before her sputtering protests could be heard. Her bag and mat had already been rolled up and tied. She dawdled over folding her discarded clothes and stuffing them into her duffel, reluctant to again face that deliberately intimate glint in Tif's gaze. He was so damned sure of himself, of his effect on her, that Andra herself could scarcely doubt he'd eventually have whatever he wanted. His attitude of familiar possessiveness would lead everyone else to think that they'd . . . Not, of course, that she cared what everyone thought, but . . .

With a shrug Andy halted the mental merry-go-round in mid-spin. It only served to make her head gyrate faster than it already was inclined to do. She left her gear piled next to Tif's and walked toward the growing babble of voices. The aromatic hiss of frying bacon tickled her nose but failed to stimulate her appetite. Although she wasn't really hungry, she joined the line at the grill and collected her breakfast plate, then sank to the ground in the first shade she could find.

Despite the very early hour the temperature climbed quickly, and Andy felt overly warm. Brushing her hair back from her brow, she could feel the heat radiate from her skin. Oddly, she wasn't perspiring. She picked listlessly at her food, then dropped her fork when a shadow crossed over her.

"Mornin', doll," said Rick cheerfully as he folded himself into place beside her. His gaze skipped swiftly past her and his mouth twisted sheepishly. "Hope you didn't mind about last night, Andy. You were sleeping soundly and . . . well, I didn't think you'd miss me. Our fearless leader said he'd take care of you."

Andra could feel her flush deepening. *Damn this heat!* she thought furiously as she retrieved her fork. She wiped the sand from it, then dropped it onto her unfinished food and shoved the plate away altogether. "No, of course I don't mind," she said in a flat voice.

Rick looked at her sharply. A frown pleated his brow, accentuating the bulldog set to his face. Andy expected him to growl at any moment. Instead, he resumed eating. When he'd swallowed the last crumb from his plate, he said with low emphasis, "If Wilson's bothering you, we'll take care of it. But, Andy . . . I like Karla. A lot. She's not the free spirit I first thought."

Now what, wondered Andy, did that mean? She regarded Rick with surprise. In all the years she'd known him, he was constantly in and out of love. Women were the delight and torment of his life, but he'd never before talked of one with quite this tone. His face was a study in serious intent.

"I like her, too," said Andy, watching him.

"She's very down-home, very real," stated Rick, almost as if seeking her disagreement. "You know what she wants to do? She wants to go rappel in Yosemite!"

It was as though he'd said Karla wanted to smother him in chocolate syrup and lick it off. He sounded ecstatic. Andy stared at him speechlessly. There was simply no understanding men. Not one of them. She grabbed her plate and stood up. "There's no problem with Tif. You just enjoy yourself and quit worrying about me."

"Sure?" he asked, walking with her.

"Positive," she replied, summoning up a smile. Where had she learned to lie like that? But she was glad she had, for Rick's face lit up with a grin and he sauntered away, whistling.

She watched his receding form with a half smile on her lips. It appeared that this time Rick Paisley had been truly smitten. She only hoped he wouldn't get hurt.

"Whatever it is you're wishing for with him, you might as well forget it," grated Tif harshly into her ear.

Jumping, Andy swiveled to face him. She held her hand over her rapidly beating heart. "You frightened me," she charged tartly.

"I'm telling you, you don't stand a chance," he went on, ignoring her accusation. "Despite your cozy little breakfast, remember he spent the night with Karla. He's fallen for her in a big way and—"

As her initial shock at being startled had worn off, she'd begun to understand what Tif was implying. She stared at his rigid face, his coldly disapproving gray eyes, and felt all her inner turmoil coalesce into one clear emotion. In a voice tremulous with anger, she interrupted abruptly. "Neither Mr. Paisley's nor my private life is a matter of your concern. You have no right to make insinuations of any kind. Nor do I want or need any of your advice."

"Give me your hand," he commanded through clenched teeth.

"What?"

He grabbed her arm and wrenched her hand upward. She made one attempt to pull it back, then stood shaking from a myriad of reasons as he brusquely squeezed ointment onto it. She was still angry. He had no right to look at her as if she were the lowest lizard in the canyon. His assumptions about her were insulting, to say the least. Yet, the heat of his fury perversely doused her own. She wanted to apologize, to explain, to soothe. The mere touch of his hand on hers, however, lodged a boulder in her throat around which no words would pass.

As soon as the gel was on her hand, he dropped it. "Rub it in," he said curtly as he capped the tube and turned away. "Then get your gear and get ready to launch."

"You should have been a Nazi commandant," she bit out beneath her breath. She didn't dare, as she longed to do, say it loud enough for him to hear. She stamped off, thinking that Carol Wilson should have been given a medal for putting up with him for as long as she had.

By the time she'd hauled her gear to the launch site and helped pick up stray litter, Andy no longer cared how angry Tif might be with her. Her only wish was to sit and do nothing until the woozy clouds cleared from her head. When Tif snapped at her to get in the first raft, she actually welcomed it. Rick and Karla climbed in the back, behind Tif, while another man got in front beside her. She looked at his white-tipped hair, his encouraging grin and vainly sought to recall his name. She offered a quavering smile in greeting, a smile which withered altogether beneath the force of Tif's reproachful glower. She closed her eyes and spent the rest of the morning trying to overcome her increasing inability to concentrate.

The constant bobbing and rocking along the hastening current did nothing to dispel Andy's light-headedness. The vertical walls of Marble Gorge hemmed her in; the winding river dizzied her. The jolting of the rapids and the incessant spray of water seemed to affect her less and less. It was as if it were happening to some other person from some faint distance. The merciless sun in the vividly clear sky seared her dry. She could not get cool. She stumbled out of the raft when told to do so, seeking only to lie down and sleep. Instead, she was handed a serving of cold cuts and a cup. She obediently sat but ignored the food.

Above the lunchtime merrymaking came the sound of engines throttling. Everyone quieted, looking upriver. Andy gazed at her plate. Why had she been given food she didn't want? There was a restless stirring around her. "What is it?" asked someone.

"Baloney boats," replied another voice close to her.

Baloney. Andra raised her head. "No, thanks, I've had enough."

Karla and Rick exchanged glances which annoyed Andy. She turned slightly away from them, looking out over the river in time to see a huge metallic-looking pontoon churn past. That was interesting. Where had she seen that before?

"Where have I seen that before?" she asked aloud.

"At the landing," answered Rick. He leaned forward, staring at her intently.

She stared back, peeved by his evasiveness. "What landing?"

"The landing at Lee's Ferry," he said slowly in the tones of one speaking to a child.

"Who's Lee?" Her question held the sharp edge of irritation. Really, they were being deliberately confusing!

The roaring noise of two more pontoons buzzed past as Karla knelt in front of Andy and tilted her chin up. As the sight and sound vanished around the next bend of the river, she called out, "Tif! I think we have a problem here." Turning to Rick, she said quickly, "Did she eat her breakfast? Did she drink anything?"

"I told you," put in Andy before Rick could, "I've had enough. I don't want baloney. Why won't you tell me who Lee is?"

She saw a pair of long, tanned legs behind Karla's shoulder, but she refused to look up. Tif's face came into view as he squatted to examine her. "Flushed face, cracked lips, no sign of perspiration," Karla was saying rapidly. "She doesn't seem to know where she is. I think she's dehydrated."

Tif swore softly. "I asked her yesterday if she'd been drinking enough liquids. Why the hell did you lie to me?" he demanded of Andra directly. "I guess lying comes naturally to a lawyer."

"Attorney. I'm an attorney," she corrected belligerently. What an insulting man, she thought, but handsome. Like a golden angel.

Some of the austerity left Tif's face. He opened the medical case, retrieved a bottle of granular powder, and mixed a spoonful into a mug of water. He handed it to Andy, and she eyed it with resentful suspicion. "It's only a mineral supplement. Now drink up or I'll be forced to pour it down your pretty little gullet."

She drank it, wondering who this man with the haloed hair thought he was. Even without knowing, she had the notion he would make good on his threat. Handing back the empty mug she demanded to know who he was. After a long hesitation, he said slowly, "I'm the man who takes care of you." To Karla and Rick he said more briskly, "Fill your canteens and make certain she drinks water every fifteen minutes. If she shows signs of any further disorientation, we'll have to lash her into the raft. Salve her lips."

When he'd handed yet another short tube to Karla, Tif walked away. Andy felt disappointed that he wasn't going to salve her lips. She meekly allowed them to lead her back to the raft, accepting their directions because she saw the blond, tanned man waiting for them. Without knowing why, she knew she wanted to be near him.

He was the one image she focused on during that interminably long afternoon. Not sure quite where she was or what she was doing, Andy did what she was told to do and steadily watched the oarsman's muscles alternately knot and relax. Occasionally, he would look over his shoulder and smile at her. She fixed on the angel-blond hair and gradually slid from consciousness.

CHAPTER SIX

Andra woke, feeling safe and secure within a warm cocoon of arms. Her contentment vanished in the instant she became aware of those arms and the rest of the body that went with them. She lay very still, deliberately slowing her breath. Without looking, she knew whose arms enwrapped her, and she didn't want to disturb Tif Wilson yet. Not until she'd figured out just what she was doing curled against him.

Feeling like Sherlock Holmes trailing a string of mystifying clues, she carefully reviewed her last remembered actions. It didn't add up to much. She recalled her extreme vertigo of the morning, her growing bewilderment. She vaguely remembered bits and pieces of the afternoon, mostly the swallowing of a great quantity of liquid. Try as she might, she couldn't recall coming to bed with Tif. She comforted herself with the thought that though he wasn't a gentleman, even Wilson wouldn't take advantage of a sick, confused woman.

Would he?

The regularity of his breathing and the heavy weight of his sleep-laden clasp convinced her she could easily slip away. Her eyes scanned the ground. Directly before her stretched a fairly clear strip of dirt. She inhaled and tensed to roll outward. Her breath expelled in a sharp gasp as Tif's clasp tightened about her waist.

"Going somewhere?" he inquired in a wickedly low whisper.

The heat of his breath tantalized her nape. She felt it cascade over her ear, then across her cheek as he turned her onto her back. He leaned above her, smiling, but even in the darkness she could see the shadow of concern.

"I guess not," she finally replied in a shaky voice.

"How are you feeling?"

"Fine. Or at least, better. Hungry."

He placed his hand on her brow, then on her neck. Her pulse leapt against his palm, then fell as he removed it. He sat up, tugging her into position beside him. Unscrewing the cap from a battered canteen, he handed it to her. "Drink a little."

"Thank you." After she'd swallowed, she handed the canteen back without looking at him. "I—I hope I wasn't too much . . . bother."

With a laugh that rustled over her skin, he shook his head. "Getting you out of the canyon in one piece may be the greatest challenge I've ever faced. Sunburn, cactus, dehydration—what do you have planned next?"

"I didn't plan—"

He cut off her indignation with a fingertip to her lip. A greasy salve covered it, and she tried to spit it back. "Don't be so damned ornery. I'm trying to save your lips from cracking any worse than they already are. I think I liked you better dazed. At least you had the sense to listen to me then."

She mumbled an apology while he greased her lips and didn't protest when he stood and hauled her to her feet. To her relief she realized she was still completely dressed, right down to her sand-spattered tennies. He wore the inevitable cutoffs but no shirt. In the moonlight his bared back gleamed darkly like flowing honey.

"Where are you taking me?" she whispered shrilly after he led her past the beached rafts, the unlit metal grill.

"What have I ever done to make you so suspicious?" he asked in reply. He suddenly stopped, and she bumped into his back. With a low chuckle he pointed her toward a scraggly clump of shrubs. "If you think you can find your way back without breaking anything, I'll go scrounge you up a sandwich."

She nodded, and he left her alone with the portable toilet. When she met him in the middle of the camp by the food containers, she greeted him with a grateful smile. He held out a sandwich, a pickle, and a mug of lemonade. In that moment Andra knew without doubt she liked Tif Wilson. Perhaps she hadn't been so fond of Theodore Wilson, but Tif was just fine.

"Thanks," she said through a mouthful of ham and cheese. "I was famished."

"So am I," countered Tif, playfully leering at her.

She decided to ignore both the leer and the instantaneous shiver along her spine. "What happened to me?"

"You got dehydrated. In this dry heat your body loses fluid without your realizing it. Perspiration dries so instantly you don't even feel the sweat."

"I'm sorry if I caused any problem."

"I'm getting used to it. You've been a constant problem from the first moment I saw you."

She choked on her ham, and he gently pounded her between her shoulder blades. Which moment did he mean? Four days ago or two years ago?

"Take, for example, the amount of sleep you've been costing me," he continued in academic tones. "The figure has spiraled nightly. By the time we reach Lava Falls, the sum of hours lost should stagger even the most hearty mathematician's soul."

"You're teasing me," accused Andy, disbelief throbbing in every word.

He laughed and Andra's heart catapulted at the tenderness of it. "Not about lost sleep. I never joke," he added suggestively, "about my time in bed."

Decidedly, Tif was not the scornful, hateful Theodore of her memories. She gazed mutely at the cast of his shadowed face, wondering how she'd failed to realize this before.

"At least the problem of lost sleep can be easily solved." He rose and again lifted her to her feet. They silently cleared the small mess they'd made, then headed back toward their bedrolls. As they walked, Tif put his arm about her waist. His fingers rested against her hip, and his thigh brushed hers with each step. Andy was surprised she didn't stumble. Her skin felt scalded, and her legs seemed too watery to hold her up, her knees too weak to bend.

When she saw the sleeping bags rolled together as one bed, she stopped in her tracks. Tif nudged her forward, then knelt by the bags and untied her shoes. She sat so he could pull them off, but didn't move when he sat beside her.

"I don't bite."

Licking her salved lips, Andy stammered, "I—I didn't think you did."

"Like I said, lying must come naturally to a lawyer." He ignored her outraged gasp to push her firmly back. "Shut up and go to sleep."

He effectively destroyed her ability to obey this order by pulling her into the crux of his arms. She could feel the steady rhythm of his heart against her back and the less steady pattern of his breath over her right cheek. Her own heart was pumping like a fire hose. Her breath was tattered. She swallowed, but her mouth was dry and only a lump of air went down.

"Tif?" she said experimentally.

"Ummm?"

His lips were dangerously close to the back of her neck. It took her three tries to speak again. "I think you should know. I—I realized tonight how—how nice you are."

There was a wonder in her tone that elicited his low rumble of laughter, stirring the short ends of hair on her nape. "Are you sure you can spare such an enthusiastic compliment, Ms. Attorney? You might deplete your stock."

"I only meant—"

"I know, I know. Go to sleep, Andy."

Stars paraded across the night, crowning the glorious tiara of the canyon rim. The muted glow of the moon eerily caressed the formidable nooks and crannies of the cliffs. Only the low murmur of the river disturbed the magical silence. Yet she could not sleep.

Andra lay folded against Tif, aching like an overeager adolescent. She wanted him, she wanted him. Not just with her body, but with her entire being. She wanted to possess and be possessed by this man who could so gently care for a woman he had every reason to resent. She wanted to feel the fullness of him. She wanted to know the completeness of him.

The undercurves of her breasts seemed to ripen where his arm rested against them. She pictured his hands and lips exploring the soft swells, the taut peaks. The image shook her to her very core. Desire threatened to overwhelm her.

In all her thirty years Andra had never faced the problem of how to tell a man she wanted him. Men had always made the invitation, and she'd either accepted or rejected. She was certain Tif still wanted her, but how did she let him know she was ready?

She listened intently. His breath was slow and even. His body lay perfectly immobile. He was asleep. She sighed heavily.

"What are you thinking?" he asked softly.

Her heart nearly jumped out of her chest. "Oh! I—you—I—" she sputtered breathlessly. "I thought you were asleep," she finally managed.

He turned her onto her back and leaned over her. Moonbeams spilled over his naked shoulders, veiling his face in darkness. After what seemed to Andy to be light-years, he placed his hand against the side of her cheek. "How could you expect me to sleep when I want you so badly it hurts?"

Unconsciously, she used a method as old as the ages to communicate her acquiescence. She quickly swiveled her head to press a kiss into the callused center of his palm, then upturned her lips in offering to his.

For a bare moment Tif hesitated. Slowly, tentatively, seeming to question her desire, he touched his mouth to hers.

That cautious kiss wrung a response from Andra that shocked her. Her body clenched with yearning, her arms automatically lifted to embrace him, her head raised to more fully accept the heady pleasure of his lips.

As he deepened the impact of their kiss, Tif slid his hands over Andra with an exquisitely soft, arousing brevity. From shoulder to breast to stomach to hip, his fingers swirled and teased and excited.

Her tension mounted as his touch lowered. She quivered with a pulsating need to know all of him. Pressing her hands flat against his chest, she delighted in each delicious ripple of the hard muscle beneath her palms. She splayed her fingers over his sinewy skin and felt the rapid hammering of his heart. The pounding beat echoed the erratic drumming of her own.

He slipped his hands under the hem of her top. She shuddered at the first sensation of his roughened fingers over her smooth flesh, then shuddered again as his hands gradually drifted up over her rib cage. No thrill of the white water could match the dizzying excitement of his tender exploration.

Abruptly, Tif pulled away from her.

Her half-closed eyes flew open. Bewildered, agonized, she parted her lips to ask him why, but no sounds came out. Even in the dim light she could see his naked hunger. His face was rigidly set, his eyes were glazed with passion. Almost afraid of the rawness of his desire, Andy looked away.

He stood. She heard the rasp of his zipper, the soft thud of denim falling onto dirt. Her wanting blazed to a desperate, searing need. She thought she would self-combust with her need of him. As he slid back down beside her, she held out her arms to eagerly embrace his nakedness.

Eluding her clasp, he lifted her arms, then tugged the terry cloth top upward. She shivered as the chilled air caressed her bare skin. He traced the laced edge of her bra with his fingertip, over one gleaming white curve, down the crescent and back over the other rounded swell. Goose bumps rose on her skin which had nothing to do with the chill of the night.

"You know," he startled her by whispering, "I never dreamed that beneath those crisply pressed suits you were this much a woman."

Before she could digest this statement, he'd nudged her prone. In the same fluid motion, he unhooked the front catch on her bra and spread it open. His rasped breath nuzzled her hardened nipples as he slid the garment off her, tossing it unseeing behind him. He leisurely flicked his tongue over her breast, tantalizing with deft, darting kisses that far surpassed any of her imaginings. He gently played with each of the pink buds in turn as he fondled the undersides with seeking hands. He kissed and caressed and roused her until she floated away on the precipitous current of desire.

As experienced as she'd believed herself to be, this

bursting, compelling, soul-consuming pleasure in his every touch, every kiss, stunned Andra. She wanted to cry out, to tell him how new, how joyous it was. Instead, she moaned softly.

When he dropped his hand to the snap on her jeans, she raised her hips to help him. He removed her clothes, then poised above her. Covered only by moonlight and Tif's shadow, Andra drew in an unsteady breath. Not wanting to do or say anything to break this rapturous spell, she paused. But the vulnerability of her nakedness solidified a vague worry, and she was forced to speak.

"Tif—"

"Shhh. This is a time for action, not words."

"But, Tif," she persisted, resisting his kiss with outstretched arms, "I need to know! Are we safe?"

He misunderstood her fear. "You aren't protected? I'll take care of it," he rasped quickly. He attempted to rise, but Andy held him back.

"No! I mean, yes. I mean, that's not what I meant."

Relaxing slowly back beside her, Tif's brows climbed in puzzlement. "What did you mean?"

"Are—are we safe from—from, you know, *things*?" She cast a wild eye over the shrubs and stones surrounding them.

So it was that they came together in laughter.

Tif curved himself over her, his body shaking with stifled mirth. The smile still clung to his lips as he kissed her, fading only when she groaned with pleasure.

The mystical beauty of the star-jeweled night enveloped them. The river's murmurous motion cadenced the pulsation of their pleasure. The cooling breeze skated over their heated bodies, heightening the warmth they took from one another. It was a night made for sharing love.

The love they shared was unlike any Andra had ever experienced. She thought she might faint from the responses Tif commanded of her. He had only to skim a finger over the shell of her ear for her body to shake with delight. His passionate persuasion of lips and tongue reduced her to liquid compliance. His masterful possession of breast and thigh raised her to unparalleled excitement.

Just when she knew she could not bear another moment of such acute sensations, Tif met her need with the driving force of his own. Feeling the hardness of him pressed within her, Andra wondered how she could have ever doubted the rightness of this. They were meant to come together like this! They were meant to share the magical wonder of one another.

Smooth and controlled, Tif continued to kiss and touch and explore the delights of Andra's body as he rhythmically prolonged their pleasure. For her, the pleasures were intense. The shattering stimulus of his hands and lips were doubled, tripled in the responses she wrung from him. The sheen of sweat oiling his straining muscles exhilarated her. The heavy catch of his ragged breath thrilled her. To know she was giving the fervent pleasure she was receiving heightened her passion beyond bearing.

When at last his control evaporated and they cascaded toward mutual ecstasy, Andy discovered a fount of fulfillment she hadn't suspected existed within her.

Amid a tangle of limbs, breathing together in a cacophony to rival the river's, Andra lay replete. She felt Tif raise his head from where he'd burrowed it in her neck to muffle his cry of satisfaction. She lazily opened her eyes when he spoke.

"That's another hour of sleep you've cost me," he whispered huskily.

"So sue me," she returned in a voice as slurred as his.

Silvered amusement streaked through eyes still heavy-lidded with gratification. He toyed with her hair, twisting and fluffing the dark strands, then he lightly kissed her brow. "Recommend any good attorneys?"

"Only one—and she's taken."

"Damn right she is," he said with a fierce possessiveness which both electrified and frightened her.

Unable to resist, she reached up and gently spread her fingertips over his forehead, brushing back the heavy layers of his startling blond hair. Moving downward, she stroked the length of his straight, pale brows. She softly swept her fingers over his narrow, downturned eyes, closing them, and down over the stubble roughening his cheeks.

She drew her hand away, then, magnetized by his masculine allure, she lightly ran her fingertip down his nose. Again and yet again, she brushed over the odd crook as if her touch would explain it.

"I don't remember this bump on your nose," she said finally.

"I didn't have it when you knew me before." Reaching up to encircle her wrist, Tif stopped her hand from retreating. Kissing the tips of her fingers, the inside of her palm, the beat of her pulse, he remarked quietly, "It's a souvenir of my temper."

A harsh note of remembered anger lay beneath his placid tone. Andy shakily released her pent-up breath. "How?"

"I got involved in a brawl in a bar. Not, I admit, what you'd expect of a mild-mannered mathematics professor—"

"Ha! You're as mild-mannered as a hungry grizzly."

He chuckled and nuzzled his mouth behind her earlobe. "Want to know what this grizzly's hungry for?"

"Want to lose another hour of sleep?" she countered pertly.

He sighed dramatically, then shrugged. "During the fight, my nose got on the wrong side of a fist, forever spoiling my handsome features."

"Not much to spoil if you ask me," she teased.

A playful slap on the curve of her rump reprimanded

her. Tif let his hand linger there, sensually stroking until Andy pushed at his hand. He was interfering with her ability to breathe. She said on a short gasp, "You're right, you know. I wouldn't expect you to fight in bars. Why did you?"

Kissing her once, he shifted his weight to her side where his face was hidden by shadows. "For the most chivalrous of motives," he said in a colorless voice which dispelled her happiness. "I was defending Carol's good name."

She lay still, feeling suffocated. She'd briefly forgotten that Carol was never far from his thoughts. Had he been thinking of Carol while making love to her? The thought stabbed so painfully, Andy looked down at her uncovered breast to see if she bled. What had been, moments before, a mystically beautiful union of two souls now appeared as nothing more than a cheap act of sexual gratification. Two people had to care, to give as well as receive, to make love. If one withheld emotion, it merely became a physical act.

Her stomach knotted. Of course he'd thought of Carol. He always thought of Carol. It had been Carol he'd first spoken of, Carol he couldn't forget no matter what the pain. While she'd been soaring in his arms, he'd been releasing himself in his memories. Humiliated and deeply hurt, Andra felt she would be sick.

As though he sensed the direction of her thoughts, Tif reached out to comfort her. She pushed roughly, earnestly at his hands. "Don't!"

He held back, and though she didn't look at him, Andy could feel his frown. "What's wrong?"

"I want to go to sleep," she lied. She started to rise, but he grabbed her arm and jerked her back down. "Let me go!"

"Not until you tell me what's wrong. What the hell did I do?" He pulled her struggling form into his arms, clamping her to his chest in an implacable grip.

She flailed uselessly against his strength, then fell limp

as she realized the fruitlessness of it. He eased his hold, and she rolled to her side, only to be yanked back to face him.

"Don't turn away from me!" he snapped, half-ordering, half-pleading.

It was the plea which calmed her. She glanced at the glitter of his eyes, then focused her gaze on his cheek. "I'm sorry, Tif. I . . . I don't think I was quite up to all this. I'm exhausted and I—I still feel sick." Actually, she felt sicker than before.

His anger vanished as quickly as it had come. He blew a soft kiss over her eyelids, then queried lightly, "Wouldn't I have made a hell of a doctor, taking advantage of the patient while she's still weak?" Telling her to wait, he left her to rummage through her duffel. She took one look at his flexing silhouette and closed her eyes. There was little sense in tormenting herself with what she had no intentions of ever again enjoying.

When he returned, he carried his gray T-shirt. "Here you are, Miss Modesty."

He bent forward to tug the shirt over her head, but Andy retreated. "Thank you," she said, taking the shirt from his hand and quickly sliding into it. He sat on his heels staring at her, but whether in anger or puzzlement she could not tell in the dark. She lay down and curled into a defensive ball, her back to his side of the bag. She heard him pick up his cutoffs and don them, then heard him stretch out beside her. It was all she could do not to weep at this dismal end to her beautiful night.

In one swift, silent movement, Tif scooped her into his arms. She gasped, and he hushed her with a kiss that drugged her into passivity. "Shhh," he murmured at the corner of her mouth. "Andra, let me hold you."

In the pause which followed, Andy envisioned their relationship tottering at the brink of a precipice as gaping as the canyon itself. Then his arms tightened convulsively, and he whispered hoarsely, "I need you." The last of her resistance melted away when he repeated in a forceful rasp, "Don't turn away from me, Andy. I need you."

She gently pressed his head against her breast. She felt the tension gradually ease from the legs and arms wrapped about hers, and slowly her own body relaxed. Her mind, however, continued to whirl furiously.

He needed her. Would it matter how, why? Would it matter if his need was to briefly forget Carol? Or even to imagine himself with her once again?

Andra sighed. His breath steadily tickled her breast, her nipple hardening to the unconscious caress. She laced her fingers into the thickness of his hair, lightly massaging his scalp while striving to sort out the turmoil raging within her.

Cheap affairs did not appeal to her. Her relationship with Tif smacked of the worst sort of one-sided affair. And yet . . . and yet, she knew in her heart that for the rest of this journey she would be his. However much Tif said he needed her, Andy knew her own need of him to be far greater. In the midst of his arms tonight, she'd suddenly understood that she'd found what she'd been searching for. The nagging dissatisfaction which had haunted her for months had simply disappeared. She had found in his arms the woman she knew herself to be, the woman she'd ruthlessly suppressed for years. Tif had brought her face to face with herself, and Andy needed him to delve into that facet of her being.

If their time together was not based on mutual love, at least they shared a mutual need.

Hugging this rationalization as she cradled Tif in her arms, Andy at last drifted into a dream-filled sleep. She dreamed about the intoxication of a kiss, the warmth of a caress, the sensuous arousal in the taste and texture of flesh meeting flesh. She dreamed about the cosmic grandeur of the canyon being ultimately realized in the sharing of heartbeats, the mingling of breaths. The awesome beauty of it was magnified; her passionate joy overwhelmingly heightened. The dream was so vivid, Andra awoke to the sound of her own low moan.

Flowing like liquid over her skin, Tif was languidly massaging the flat plane of her stomach and the swell of her hips. He imprinted a kiss on the hollow of her throat. Andy heard herself mew and came fully awake.

"What—" she began, only to have her words stolen by his lips. He lifted his head to smile at her. "Are—" she tried again. He once again firmly silenced her. "You doing?" she finished breathlessly several moments later.

He straddled her full length. Now, he raised himself on his elbows and smiled intimately down at her. At the smoky intent in his eyes, her heart changed cadence, flipping wildly.

"You know," he mused conversationally, "poor ol' Prince Charming hasn't been given enough credit for the power of his kiss. This prince gave up trying to awaken his Sleeping Beauty with a mere kiss twenty minutes ago."

Beneath her sunburn, her cheeks tingled with a rush of color. She remembered the intensity of her dream, and she trembled beneath the solid weight of him.

"Well, I'm awake now," she pointed out while trying not to shake. "So, if you'll just get off me—"

"Haven't you heard of a man enjoying the fruits of his labors? As pleasurable as those labors have been"—he kissed her roundly on the lips—"I'm certain the fruits will bear even more delight."

His hand was lifting the T-shirt. Andra's pulse sped. "But what if someone awakens and—"

"What of it? Why would it matter?" She didn't know how to reply, and after a short pause, he continued in a thickened tone, "Let me share the dawn with you. I want to see by the morning light what I felt in the moonlight last night. I want to see you responding to me, Andra."

She couldn't argue with such persuasive logic. Not that she was crazy enough to try. She curled her legs around his calves, raised her arms, and arched her body toward him.

"What you see," she murmured raggedly, "is what you get."

With a deep groan, Tif lowered himself to her. He cradled her head between his palms and showered her face with endless kisses. The intensity of each spiraled until the sensation melted all restraint. Soon, her clothes tangled with his in a discarded heap. They felt and tasted and together plumbed new depths as they recaptured their moonlit enchantment.

Long, lazy fingers of sunlight reached out over massive walls of brilliant ruby and gold to embrace them. Andra could clearly see what had been hidden from her the night before. The morning light unveiled the need darkening Tif's eyes, the restless longing set rigidly over his features, and the transformation as pleasure transported him to fulfillment. She saw, and her own passion escalated to new heights.

Determined not to mar the magical wonder she felt, Andy lay silently listening as Tif's breath slowed and evened. Whatever his reasons—or hers—such joyous coming together could not be wrong. For her, at least, they'd transcended the physical, and nothing, no one, and especially no memory would be allowed to ruin it.

He stirred above her, shifting until he gazed down at her with molten contentment. "Andra—"

Her hands flew up to press against his mouth. *Don't spoil this!* her eyes widened to plead. He tenderly kissed her fingertips, then, as she'd known he would, her lips.

"Honey—" he breathed over the curve of her mouth.

Once again, she effectively muted his attempt to speak. He was not, she noted happily, entirely loath to being maneuvered in this manner. She lightly raked her nails down his naked back and delighted in his shudder.

It was her turn to tremble as he slid his palms from her hips up over her breasts. Lingering to tease her responsive nipples with his hands, he bent his head to nibble on her earlobe. "My sweet," he whispered as he flicked his tongue behind her ear, "I want you to look at one of nature's most stunning works of abstract art."

A knowing smile spread languidly over her lips. He certainly thought highly of himself! Slowly lifting her eyelids, she murmured her assent. To her surprise he turned her head to the side, pressing his cheek against hers. At the edge of the sleeping bag, running diagonally toward the head of it, was a long, thin, rippling line in the sand.

He dropped a kiss on the tip of her nose, then answered the question in her eyes. "Snake tracks," he said succinctly.

It took one second for it to sink in, less than a fraction of that for her to react. Shoving his weight aside, Andra catapulted from the bag. Hopping on first one foot, then the other, she sputtered in rage, "Why didn't you *tell* me! You—you—oh!"

Tif sat upright, shoulders heaving as he roared with uninhibited laughter. Andy stood stock-still, her outrage and fear forgotten. Sunshine glinted silver over tousled blond hair and gleamed bronze over deeply tanned muscles. Crinkles accentuated the downward droop of his sparkling eyes and tilted beside his squared lips. Laughter transformed him completely.

Andra stood and stared and saw Tif as she'd never seen him before. What she saw shook her from head to toe.

She saw a man she wanted to love.

CHAPTER SEVEN

The river began to flex its muscles. Churning like an angry melted chocolate malt, the Colorado threw huge brown waves, wildly whirling eddies, powerfully sweeping currents, at the small convoy of rafts. The further they traveled, the more frequently the boatmen pulled ashore to study the river and confer before pushing off into the heart of the thundering rapids. Pounding and tossing, the rapids challenged ever more vigorously.

As the river changed, so did the canyon. Bejeweled towers of rock became a forbidding narrow gorge of jagged gray and black crags. The cliffs rose sheer from the water's edge, obscuring all view of the outer world beyond a ribbon of azure sky. Several times the river seemed to crash straight into solid canyon wall, each sharp turn hidden until they clamored around it. Along the way indirect sunlight reflected seams of pink granite threaded within the black walls, lightening the lonely eeriness of Granite Gorge and precisely matching the rosy glow of Andy's mood.

And, she thought, peering squint-eyed into the mirror she'd borrowed from Nancy, it duplicated the hue of her burned skin. She frowned at the image of her peeling nose, then paused, arrested by the face staring back at her. How on earth could Tif describe her, as he had in a hoarse love-whisper at daybreak, as breathtaking? Unless he'd meant the sight of her made him gag for air.

She laughed aloud. Really, she'd never looked less appealing in her life. In place of her usual immaculately styled curls was a rumpled, windswept ash-brown mop. Her long fingers no longer ended in gloriously manicured nails. Two more had broken; the rest were hopelessly split and chipped. Her reddened skin glistened with lotions and gels; her chapped lips sported a coat of salve. Only her eyes were lovelier than before. They seemed wider, brighter, with an incandescent sparkle illuminating the brown depths. All of her brilliant happiness glittered in her eyes.

She would not, six days ago, have believed such inner radiance possible. But two nights and two dawns shared with Tif Wilson had dazzled her. She'd been astonished by his tender control the first night and even more so by his trembling eagerness last night. Above all, she'd been shaken by her own shattering responses to him. No man had ever taken her to such searing heights, nor cared so much for her pleasure as well as his own.

Thinking about it, Andy quivered. She lowered the mirror and sought the figure of the man whose touch made her feel so alive. Sweeping over the Phantom Ranch ranger station, her gaze flicked impatiently past the teary embraces exchanged between the departing coeds and the men who were remaining. They'd put in at the ranch to let off those who'd only signed up for the first portion of the river journey and to welcome those who'd hiked down the trail from the South Rim to join them. Andy looked beyond the shifting scene of wayfarers, eyes searching.

His sun-bleached hair made him easy to locate. Tif was amidst a cluster of new passengers, demonstrating the fastening of the life jackets. As she watched, a vision flashed of that blond hair bent over her, brushing her breast as he brought himself to her. Again, she shivered.

"Are you feeling okay?" asked Karla, who sat beside her.

"Never better," answered Andy truthfully. Though she'd still suffered some discomfort the day before, she now felt completely recovered from the effects of her dehydration. Despite the sunburn and the sting of her injured hand, she was filled with a sense of well-being. She reluctantly tore her gaze from Tif to grin at the brunette. "I've actually made it through twenty-four hours without doing any further damage to myself, which must be a record. If I only live to make it back to my safe little apartment, away from the dangers of the wild, I'll stay there."

A knowing glint skated through Karla's blue eyes as she glanced once at Tif, then past Andy. Looking up at the South Rim, she continued to plait her hair into a pair of dark braids. "Whether you believe it or not, by the end of this trip you'll be a bona fide outdoor adventurer. I think you'll find that you've been bitten. You'll want to do something like this again."

"Oh, no, I won't. Just because I was crazy enough to let Rick drag me on this trip doesn't mean I'm insane enough to do it again." But even as she said it, Andy couldn't refrain from looking at Tif and wondering. Would she come back if he asked her to? Not ready to admit that she would, she quickly averted her gaze and transferred her attention to the pair standing a few feet from Tif's group.

Her eyes widened, then narrowed as she watched the southern dentist enfold the slim figure of the college girl. He stood facing the newcomers, his arms wrapped around the girl and his hands rubbing her buttocks. But his gaze was fastened on a pair of long, smooth legs descending from beige hiking shorts hugging the slim hips of a new passenger. He inched his eyes up over the young woman buckling her life jacket, clearly, coolly, assessing each curve. All the while he was murmuring in the coed's ear, running his hands over her.

Icy cold fingers slid down Andy's spine. She saw herself embracing Tif, whispering broken farewells, while Tif coolly examined the next woman to share the river with him.

Jumping up, Andy excused herself to Karla and walked swiftly away from the tormenting sight of the dentist and his games. Tif wouldn't play games with her, he wouldn't! What they'd had the past two days was too special to doubt. She would not allow herself to sour their relationship over any what-might-comes.

She found Nancy complaining to her brother Larry over the heat. With a tight expression of thanks, Andy returned the mirror and quickly moved on. She wanted to be alone to think. That's why she'd come on this damn trip in the first place, wasn't it? And what had she accomplished? Nothing!

Unless you counted complicating her confusion with a king-sized infatuation for a man incapable of reciprocating her feelings.

Infatuation? Andra stopped. Tugging on the loose flaps of her life jacket, she certainly hoped it was nothing more than that. She knew she could all too easily fall in love with Tif. He was everything she'd ever wanted in a man. Gentle, yet strong. Tender, yet firm. Even his short-fused temper seemed lovable to her now. But she knew she must not allow herself to do so. He would never love her in return. . . .

A pair of arms slid around her waist, startling her. Chuckling, Tif whirled her around. Looking into her widened eyes, his smile faded. "What's wrong, sweetheart? Aren't you feeling well? You've been drinking enough liquids, haven't you?"

"I'm fine," she said quickly. "I—you just took me by surprise. As usual."

He wasn't to be put off. Tilting her head back, he examined her eyes, her cheeks, her lips, while his fingers circled her wrist to monitor her pulse. "You're sure?"

She smiled, her discontent melting away in the heat of his concern. "I'm sure. I've been drinking enough water to qualify as a tank."

"I don't want you passing out on me again. . . ."

"If I'm looking sick, it's left over from Hance Rapid," she teased. "I saw my life flash before my eyes back there."

"If we weren't surrounded by tourists and park rangers, I'd kiss you so dizzy you wouldn't have wits left to be frightened with."

Her heart kicked. Oh, god, she wanted him! She wanted him in a trembling way that only seemed to spiral. The more she had, the more she wanted. She licked her lip and saw his eyes darken as his gaze followed the motion.

His clasp on her wrist tightened. "Do you know what you're doing to me? I'd like to dump this entire load of passengers on someone else and carry you off into the canyon and love you senseless."

"I thought you'd taken care of my senses this morning," she whispered, her voice dropping seductively.

"I'll show your senses a thing or two tonight."

"Is that a promise?"

He caught his breath, then finally let her wrist go and spun round. "It's time to put in," he said over his shoulder.

She looked down at her wrist. A white bracelet stood out against the red of her skin. She was certain there would be a bruise. He'd left his mark on her. It was this streak of intense possessiveness which had so disturbed Carol. It had, at the time, disturbed Andra on Carol's behalf. Finding herself the object of it now, however, had quite another effect. An acute thrill shot through her, pulsing in her veins, beating in her heart. He may not love her, but Tif wanted her as badly as ever he'd wanted any woman.

The knowledge buoyed her so much that she didn't feel the least tremor when Tif, for the benefit of the newcomers, reviewed the procedure should a boat flip over. In truth, she wasn't so very fearful of the river anymore. The day before had passed without incident, and though Hance today had been rough, her confidence in Tif's ability to get them through it had given her the courage to enjoy the fright. She climbed into the back of the lead raft with an assured smile, settling back to watch the action of Tif's powerful muscles as he plied the oars.

Two of the new passengers got in front, a retired couple who looked remarkably alike. Their eyes twinkled and crinkled in the same way, and their lips lifted in twin smiles. Andy greeted them cheerfully, ignoring her secret pang of envy as she saw them exchange an intimate glance. How lucky to grow old with someone you loved, graying together, sharing memories of laughter and tears over the years. She pushed the intrusive reflection away to listen to the slim boy from Brooklyn, Brent Delcado, telling the older couple about the Grand Canyon.

"It's as wide as seven Golden Gate Bridges linked together and spans the distance from London to Paris in length. The guide book I bought says that it's one of only three places in the world where we get back to rocks two or three billion years old."

His enthusiasm made the rest of them smile broadly. They drifted along, Tif rowing, Brent talking, and Andra lazily regarding the black-throated swifts which coasted close to the water. She heard the familiar distant roar, rather like a muted sports crowd, then saw the water drop into the unknown. Her knees no longer knocked together at the sight. She actually parted her lips to ask Tif which rapid they were entering when he abruptly stood, then sat quickly and ordered tersely, "Hold on."

Andy barely had time to clutch at the nylon gear strap when the raft plunged sideways down a deep descent, then slammed up into a sheer wall of water. Waves violently punched them on all sides, accelerating them into another, more forcefully swirling current. Bucking like a slow motion bronco, the raft plowed through another standing cascade of raging water. Frantically, Andy gripped the strap as they headed for yet another towering haystack wave.

Without warning, the nylon snapped free of the raft. Andy was thrown backward. She felt herself inevitably flipping over the side and knew she was about to meet death head-on. As waves jabbed at her rib cage, a pair of arms tackled her legs, hanging on to her sodden jeans. Expecting immersion in freezing water, she'd shut her eyes. Now they wrenched open. Sprawling against her legs, his bushy hair damped down as the river sprayed over them, Brent grinned at her and called out, "Wow! Wasn't that *great?*"

Great was not the term she would have chosen, but she managed a feeble smile in gratitude of having had her life saved. She remained in shaken silence as they bailed, refusing to look back as the other rafts charged through Horn Rapid. In those few terrifying fragments, she'd remembered why she hadn't wanted to come on this trip. When all five crafts pulled ashore a mile downriver from Horn, Andy staggered out, thankful to be on dry land.

"My dear, how *very* thrilling for you!" exclaimed the grandmotherly Edna Wardice as she came up behind Andy. "Oren and I were so *surprised* when you flew backward. Why, when we looked back, we thought for sure you were going out of the raft!"

"So did I," said Andy flatly, though she tried to return Edna's smile. Noting the older woman's sopping flowered blouse and knit slacks, she said more kindly, "You'd better get your gear and change into something dry."

Edna patted Andy's arm. "Don't you be worrying about me. Oren does enough of that! You just go change your own things, my dear, and we'll see you over supper."

Her husband smiled encouragingly at Andy, then the two walked away, arm in arm. She shivered, chilled from the frigid drenching she'd received, but she knew a change of clothes wouldn't warm her. She was chilled through and through. Her fright on the river had compounded her earlier disquiet. This whole trip was one misfortune after another, not the least of which was her deplorable attraction to Tif Wilson.

Tif disappeared the instant they landed. This unreasonably angered Andy. She took it as a sign that he didn't care about her near-disaster, that he didn't give a damn about what happened to her. Still feeling rattled, and not a little sorry for herself, Andy forced her wobbly legs to move, joining the crowd waiting for gear to be unpacked and distributed. When Rick Paisley stopped her to ask where she and Tif would be bedding down, she snapped, "What makes you think we're bedding down together?"

Taken aback, Rick mumbled, "Well, I—I just assumed—"

"Assumed?" parroted Andy, her voice rising irrationally. "Well, you can just stop assuming! I'd sooner bed down with—with—that raging rapid back there. Which I nearly did, but no one seems to give a damn about that."

Rick began edging away from her, pulling at his sparse hair with one beefy hand while placating her with the other. "Sorry, Andy. I didn't mean to upset you. I'll talk to you later, okay? When you're feeling more like yourself."

"I do feel like myself. For the first time in several days, I feel exactly like myself," she retorted. But Rick had already retreated, and her words fell on empty air.

Once she'd towed her sleeping roll and duffel to a high spot hidden behind two huge black boulders, she realized that although she'd been unfair to Rick, she'd spoken no less than the truth. For the first time in days, since she'd suffered the delirium of dehydration, in fact, she felt like herself. The game she'd been playing with Tif was nothing more than that. An elaborate game, enacted time and time again by the travelers down the river. Well, she had no intention of continuing the charade. If he wanted amusement, let him compete with the dentist for Miss Legs, she thought as she gave her duffel a furious little kick.

"What did that poor bag ever do to you?" drawled an amused voice behind her.

Wheeling, Andy faced Tif with a heavy frown. "Go away," she said coldly.

The smile he wore shriveled. With a heavy sigh he dropped his bag and roll into the sand beside hers. "Now what's wrong?"

"Nothing is wrong. I just want to be left alone, that's all. So please go find yourself somewhere else to sleep."

"Sleeping wasn't exactly what I had in mind."

She gasped. How dare he make such suggestions when he hadn't even cared whether she fell into the river or not! Glaring, she declared with emphasis, "It's the only thing on my mind, I can assure you. So please go."

He didn't move. His face set rigidly and his eyes narrowed as he steadily regarded her. "What is it with you, anyway?" he asked after a long silence. "Back at Phantom Ranch you weren't thinking about sleep tonight. Far from it."

"Well, I'm thinking about it now," she muttered, lying. She wished he would go away and leave her alone. She didn't need him to make her feel any more miserable than she already was.

Unable to meet his gaze, Andy became absorbed in the drawstrings on her duffel bag. She could feel his eyes boring through her and had to work not to visibly tremble. The sand crunched beneath his feet as he pivoted and took a step. Of their own volition, her eyes raised. In that instant he wheeled round to face her, eyes flinty and without warmth.

"That first night I had you pegged as a tease," he said in a low tone full of hostility. He ignored her objection to continue ruthlessly, "But for a while there you had me fooled into believing otherwise. I have been a gigantic fool, haven't I, Andra? It's only now occurred to me that you've been continuing the game you and Carol began together. Wasn't it enough that you took your pound of flesh during my divorce proceedings?"

"That's not true!" she denied heatedly. "You were the one who inflicted the pain by playing games, not Carol!"

"Leave her out of this," he ordered through tight lips.

Ignoring him, she went on heatedly, "You're the one who drew out the proceedings inch by bitter inch; you're the one who drove Carol to a near-breakdown; you're the—"

"This has nothing to do with Carol!" he cut in sharply. The angry voice she remembered so well now rumbled full-steam. "Or me. We are talking about *you*, Ms. James, you and your sport. I don't give a damn who else you might toy with once you're out of this canyon, but I'm telling you now, counselor, for the good of this camp, cut out the games."

"I haven't been playing games!" she burst out, but he was already striding away and gave no indication that he heard.

He hadn't touched her, and yet Andy felt as if she'd been brutally struck. Bracing herself against one of the boulders, she swallowed several deep, painful breaths. Damn him! A week ago she'd been a calm, collected, coolheaded person. Now she was behaving like the worst sort of immature adolescent. She might as well have run herself through a Vegematic as to spend six days on the river with Tif Wilson! No wonder Carol had been in such a state. . . .

At the thought of Carol, Andy remembered Tif's angry accusations. Had he really believed she and Carol plotted against him? How could he think she'd be capable of such things? He could because where Carol was concerned, Tif was unable to think rationally. The mere mention of her touched him on the raw and ignited his explosive temper. His continuing love for his ex-wife clouded his judgment.

Just as, thought Andy with a plummeting heart, her own judgment had vanished from the moment she'd seen him back at Lee's Ferry. She now saw that she'd skipped infatuation and gone straight to love.

The conclusion staggered her. She sank to sit cross-legged in the sand. Frowning at the gear Tif had left behind, Andy asked herself how it had happened. How had she fallen in love in the space of a few days? She who'd devoted herself to her career, for whom men had provided passing pleasure. No man had ever meant enough to cause Andy a moment's pain.

No man except Tif Wilson.

She supposed she'd always been attracted to him. Two years before, his volatile temperament and Carol's distress had obscured her own inclinations. Given the opportunity to see the other facets of Tif—his humor, his gentleness, his depth of character—away from Carol's bias, Andra's attraction had quickly blossomed into something far more significant. It was this, of course, which led her to so hastily lose her temper with him, so swiftly find fault. She could release her pent-up emotions in argument. Hadn't Tif always done the same with Carol?

Whatever happened the rest of the trip, Andy vowed not to let Tif know how she truly felt. One-way love too easily could become twisted. She knew he'd been drawn to her because of her connection to Carol and not because of any real feelings for herself. For him their relationship was purely a physical thing.

Feeling she'd done enough soul-searching for one day, Andy stood and brushed the sand from her still-damp clothes. She rejoined the rest of the group and went through the motions of helping to set up camp, searching for firewood, then wrapping potatoes in foil for baking over the grill. All the while, she was vividly aware of being palpably ignored by Tif. The few occasions their eyes met by chance, his slid distastefully over her before moving on to something more worthy of viewing. It left her feeling empty, yet she didn't really blame him. The argument had been her fault, and she must accept the consequences.

She was standing between Penny Jacobson and one of the new campers, a reedy teenager named Robin, drying dishes and discussing the day's run on the river when the first crack of thunder sounded. The trio jumped in union, then looked beyond the rim's jagged edge. What minutes before had been a clear cerulean sky was now darkly crowded with looming clouds. With the second booming, the wind gathered to rush over them, swirling sand in all directions.

Those who'd brought tents scattered to raise them. Andy sent Penny and Robin off, assuring them she could finish wiping the few remaining plates. When she'd dried the last of them, she helped Mike pack them away, then at last headed for her gear. As she passed Rick and Karla setting up their tent, Karla called out an invitation to share with them. Calling out her thanks, she hurried on. The wind was gusting now, and fingers of lightning darted through the heliotrope of the sky.

Every passenger had been given a voluminous plastic poncho at the outset of the trip. Andy extracted this from her duffel and hastily drew it on, pulling the hood up over her hair. Dragging the bag behind her, she started back to join Rick and Karla just as the storm swooped down in earnest. Sand and rain flew up into her face, and she stumbled as she instinctively shut her eyes.

She was grasped from behind and shoved forward. The hood acted as a blinder, preventing her from seeing anything except that she was being propelled into a small pup tent. She fell on her knees. The duffel landed with a plop beside her. Her sleeping bag lay open within the tiny space, and with shock she recognized the bag spread next to it.

"You might as well remove your poncho and get comfortable," said Tif as he fastened the tent flap closed. "It looks like we'll be in here a long while."

His voice was neither friendly nor welcoming. It was totally blank. Her eyes adjusted slowly to the opaque interior. Beneath the bellow of the wind, she heard the hushed movement as he slid back to sit beside her. Her heart began to pound. There was no room for her to escape being less than a few feet away from him. She couldn't even stand up within the small space. She'd never before suffered claustrophobia, but she felt overwhelmingly closed in now.

Spectral shadows leapt in a macabre dance as Tif switched on a lantern flashlight. Andy blinked into the blinding beam, then away. To her dismay Tif's presence was visible wherever she looked. Out of the corner of her eye she saw him kick free of his Nikes, pushing them into the shadows. She saw the fine dusting of golden hairs down the length of his legs; she saw the lazy flex of his toes.

"You'll roast if you don't take off that poncho," he said, sounding rather as if the notion of roasted Andra gave him enormous pleasure.

"I wouldn't want to be accused of *teasing* you with my charms," she snapped sarcastically before she could stop herself. Damn it, she'd meant to be conciliatory and very, very reasonable with him!

"Oh, believe me, there isn't the least chance of it. There has to be an interest on the part of the victim before a tease can succeed."

The mockery in his voice pricked at her. She forgot her resolution to remain mature and sensible. Shedding the poncho and dropping it into a dark corner, she said with childish ill will, "Sticks and stones won't hurt me. I can only hope the rain will spare me by letting up soon."

The canvas groaned against the wind's assault and rattled beneath the steady pelting of the now-pouring rain. Each clash of thunder reverberated through the gorge. Stilted silence echoed within the tent.

Tif stretched out full-length on his bag, hands folded beneath his head. Andy sat as erectly as she could, her legs cramping from being crossed for so long. But she wasn't going to lay down beside him!

Was he asleep? His breathing seemed to fill the silence. It was steady and slow, not at all like her own nervous puffs. His shirt, unbuttoned as usual, had fallen open. In the thin strip of light his chest gleamed, the skin bronzed and glowing with health. Andy refused to notice it.

If he was asleep, there was no sense in her continuing to crink her neck and stiffen her tired muscles. She tentatively straightened her legs. He didn't move. She slid downward, careful to avoid touching him. When she was prone beside him, she let out a long, drawn-out sigh of relief.

"I hear you had a misadventure today," commented Tif.

She sprang upward, knocked against an aluminum pole at her feet, and fell backward as the end of the tent crumpled in a flattened heap. She kicked uselessly against the heavy canvas shrouding her legs, struggling to sit back up.

"Damn it, stay still and let me get this damn thing back in position," directed Tif curtly.

He crawled over her legs, groping for the pole and

rubbing over much of her lower anatomy as he did so. Feeling the warmth of his flesh, Andy involuntarily jerked, accidentally throwing her knee against his groin. He doubled over, grunting in pain.

"Oh, my god, I'm sorry!" she exclaimed, distressed. Reacting without thought, she thrust herself upright and reached out blindly. "Let me—" she cried as her flailing arms bumped the pole at the tent's head, "—help."

Layers of canvas muffled her plea beneath the collapsing tent. It did nothing, however, to stifle Tif's angry rasp. "Don't move! Don't move . . . one . . . goddamned . . . muscle."

It was a command to be obeyed. Andra did as she was told, chewing on her lower lip and adding her own mental castigations to the colorful curses Tif was heaping on her head. The canvas was smothering her, but she didn't dare complain. She didn't even dare to apologize. She lay still as he maneuvered into a kneeling position at her feet and hoped he didn't hate her too much.

Uttering a string of oaths, Tif raised the end pole, then sprawled over Andy to position himself at the head pole. The weight and scent and flexure of him filled her senses. She longed to spread her fingers over the muscles so tantalizingly near. But she didn't so much as draw a breath for fear of again hurting him. When he managed to undo the flap and crouch outside to lift the pole, she allowed herself to take in a deep, if shaky, breath.

Hearing another vivid curse, Andy dared to shift toward the flap and peer out. Lightning streaked, intensely illuminating the canyon's primeval darkness and outlining Tif where he stood restaking one corner of the tent. A blast of wind carried a stream of water inward, liberally spattering Andy. She retreated to dig through her duffel, extracting a towel. She paused, then pulled out another. She held it out wordlessly to Tif as he reentered.

He secured the flap, then squatted beside her. As he

took the towel from her outstretched hand, their fingers touched. Each jerked back. Andy stared fixedly at the puddle forming around Tif's dripping body. She felt as if a lightning bolt had reached out to shock her. She didn't move as Tif ruffled his drenched hair with the towel. Holding it before his face, he gazed over the cloth at her.

"The next time you want to help, do me a favor and don't."

That stirred her into gaping wide-eyed at him. She was unable to believe she'd heard the amusement in his voice, but when he dropped the towel to begin wiping his chest, she saw the glimmer of his grin. He shrugged out of his wet shirt and began to unzip his cutoffs. She quickly turned her back to him.

"Modesty again?" he queried with a low chuckle. "There isn't anything you haven't already seen."

She ignored him. He reached across her and she jumped. He flicked the flashlight off. The sudden curtain of night enveloped them with a hush. The rustling of his discarded denims seemed to ring in Andy's ears. In a ghostly display, the white of the towel illusively glinted as it whisked over his body. Andra had difficulty breathing as she watched it move ever lower. A longing to touch him as that towel touched him throbbed within her. Finally, the towel fell to the floor, and Tif once again stretched out over his bag. After hesitating a moment, Andy did the same.

"Have you always been this accident-prone?" he provokingly inquired.

Andra deliberately turned on her side, presenting him with a shoulder colder than an Arctic cap.

"Wouldn't you be more comfortable out of your wet clothes?"

"I'm fine just as I am."

They lay in the darkness, listening to the rain and the wind and each other's clamoring heartbeat. Andy shifted restlessly. She tried, but failed, to steady her nerves. The picture of his nakedness raced up and down her body, raising goose bumps along the way.

"So tell me what happened today," said Tif finally.

This time she didn't jump. She'd expected something, though she had no idea what. Tame conversation, however, wasn't it.

"You must know, or you wouldn't ask." A hint of accusation underscored her words.

"I know what Edna Wardice told me, but I wondered how much was fact and how much exaggeration. She said you were nearly swept into the river back at Horn and that Brent saved you." He waited for her to say something but then went on. "I checked the strap on the raft and had Steve mend it."

He hadn't known! Well, if she'd been thinking clearly she'd have realized his attention was focused on maneuvering through the rapids, not on the passengers, especially not the two behind him. It had all been over in a matter of seconds. By the time they'd gotten out of the rapids, she'd been righted and had begun to bail. Feeling guilty and embarrassed, Andy haltingly explained her mishap. Tif probed, deftly extracting the aftereffects, the fear and anger she'd felt.

Again the silence expanded between them, punctuated by the steady downpour outside. Again Andy took herself to task for jumping to conclusions and spoiling what little time she'd have had with Tif. Again, just when she was certain he'd fallen asleep, he startled her.

Moving before she had time to react, he rolled over on top of her, pinning her beneath him. "Is that what was behind our argument? Is it?"

"Yes," she admitted on a thin whisper. She felt about an inch high, knowing herself to have been in the wrong. She expected him to swing away from her in disgust, but he surprised her by pressing his palms against her cheeks and kissing her brow.

"For a smart attorney you can be one stupid lady," he murmured, kissing her eyelids. "How the hell was I supposed to know what had happened? Look, Andra, we can't solve anything if I don't know what it is I've done. I don't mind having you mad at me—" He paused and chuckled. "Well, maybe I do mind, but the point is, if we're arguing, we both have to know why or nothing is going to get settled."

Her hands fluttered against his chest. He raised slightly, and she lifted them to his shoulders. "I know. I'm sorry," she said breathlessly. He tickled her earlobes with the tips of his fingers, and she was having difficulty thinking. "Did I . . . hurt you . . . too much?"

He nipped on the edge of her lip. "A little harder, my sweet klutz, and you'd have ended the Wilson line."

"I'm sorry, I—"

"All apologies accepted," he interrupted briskly. "Now tell me what was wrong today."

"It's just . . . I came on this trip to . . . to find myself. . . . What are you doing?" she broke off to ask as he began undoing her shirt.

"I'm undressing you." He leisurely stroked her collarbone, warmly nuzzled his mouth along her jawline, and eventually loosened another button. "So are you finding yourself?"

"No . . . I'm more . . . lost . . . than ever," she gasped.

He bared her breasts and burrowed his lips between them. "In order to find something, it has to be lost," he said while dropping a light kiss over each nipple. "Perhaps you weren't lost enough to find yourself." His hands slid down to her hips, circling over the denim before moving to the snap.

Tugging on his hair, she pulled his mouth back up to

hers, silencing him. This was, in her estimation, no time to be philosophizing over her personal problems.

He lifted his head to gaze down at her. "Promise me one thing, Andra," he commanded with one of his endearing rumbled laughs.

"What?" she panted, wanting him to hurry, wanting him.

"Promise me you'll endeavor not to knock the tent down while we're making love."

CHAPTER EIGHT

The click of Rick's camera was drowned out by the continuous crashing of Crystal Rapid. Tormented waves beat against the sunbaked boulder upon which Andra stood waiting with the other passengers. After a brief consultation with the other boatmen, Tif had ordered them to portage themselves around the rapid while the oarsmen alone navigated the dangerously low waters. Heart in mouth, Andy watched Tif maneuver his boat through the inhospitable rapids. His raft folded in two as it was swept up on a heaving wave and swung toward shore. For one interminable moment she was certain he would smash into the very rock on which she stood. Then, impossibly, the raft slid safely by.

When the other rafts had negotiated the run, the passengers scrambled down the rock to meet them ashore. Tif was grinning and exchanging quips with Mike. "You almost shaved your mustache off on that boulder." He was laughing as Andra joined him.

His humor annoyed her. He could have been hurt back there! "How can you make jokes?" she demanded in a furious whisper. "You almost hit the rocks yourself. You could have been killed!"

He smiled indulgently, the conquering hero comforting the little woman. Andra ground her teeth. "I told you, the river's safer than any freeway in the nation. In all the years of commercial rafting—more than twenty-five years—only two people have ever died as a direct result of the rapids. That's out of hundreds of thousands of people."

It was hollow comfort. But if he wanted to laugh in the face of death, that was his problem. She certainly didn't intend to worry about him. She scowled heavily, and his smile deepened.

"I'm flattered you're so concerned about me," he said as he guided her into the raft.

"I'm merely concerned about having to row my own raft if you ever get hurt," she retorted, hoping he didn't know how she lied.

Since the rain-driven reconciliation of the night before, Andy feared that Tif already knew how much she cared, and why. If he did, there was nothing she could do about it. She was simply determined to milk as much joy from the rest of their trip together as she could. She'd worry about her unrequited future when the time came and not one second before. So wearing a glittering smile for Tif's benefit, she climbed into the raft along with Rick, Karla, and the teenaged Robin.

Snowy egrets skimmed through the air, performing a graceful aerial ballet for the canyon intruders. Rick started a word game, which they played amid groans and laughter for the rest of the afternoon. Andra sat up front, and each time she turned her head Tif's gaze glittered over her. Each time, the tempo of her pulse thrust into dynamic speeds.

The lead raft's mood for merrymaking affected the entire camp. Over a tasty supper of grilled pork chops and buttered peas, someone began a round of "When I came on this trip, I packed the one thing I couldn't leave behind, my—" Some of the answers were sensible, some silly, some lewd, and some very insightful. Tif had said, "My oars," and Andy, "My first-aid kit." Oren Wardice drew a large round of laughter when he responded with "My wife."

From across the campfire Howard Jacobson called out, "This was the one thing you couldn't leave behind, not the thing you wanted to." Knowing laughter and whistles again shrilled, and the game moved on. But Penny shot him a glare from behind her glasses and said loudly, "Very amusing, Howie."

"I thought so," he returned shortly.

"It's too bad your attempts at humor aren't half so amusing as your attempts at lovemaking," she hissed. She flicked her short auburn coils back with her hand for emphasis.

"If you'd try not to have one of your oh-so-convenient headaches, maybe my technique would improve."

"You can't improve what you don't have—and believe me, you don't have any technique." Penny lowered her voice, but their bickering continued with pointedly sharp barbs exchanged between sips of beer.

To the left of them, Tif leaned to whisper in Andy's ear, "Let's get out of here." He stood, then lifted her to her feet, and they strolled toward their bedrolls. "I hope you didn't mind, but I'd about had enough of that."

Glancing at his set face, she said tentatively, "The Jacobsons' argument bothered you, didn't it?"

One of his shoulders tilted in a dismissive shrug. "Not particularly. They just forgot which game they were playing, that's all. When they began playing marital dispute, I thought we would do as well to leave."

"Marital dispute?"

"It's one of the more particularly ugly aspects of marriage. I've been through enough rounds to consider myself an expert, but I've vowed never to do so again. I didn't see why we should be forced to watch another couple stick it to each other."

They walked on wordlessly. Tif had sounded embittered. It depressed Andra to think how soured he'd been. Soured enough never to marry again. Behind them she could hear the hum of voices sprinkled with occasional laughter, and on sudden impulse she halted to gaze up at his shadowed face.

"Did you and Carol argue a lot?"

Her heart galloped into the silence as she awaited his reply. After what seemed an eon, he said tonelessly, "Not at first, no. I met her at the university in Columbia. She was a student majoring in journalism with an emphasis on media technique. I was a graduate assistant in the math department. We got along in those days."

"What went wrong?"

"We'd been married about a year when she got her first job. It wasn't even as if she needed to work. I'd been hired at UMKC and was making enough to support us."

Andra expelled her breath sharply. "Just because she'd gotten married was no reason for her not to fulfill herself in other ways. That's a very selfish, repressive attitude."

"You have me cast as the villain of our marriage, don't you? The male chauvinist who felt threatened by a successful female, is that it?"

"If the shoe fits," she returned tartly.

"I don't happen to think it does, but that's probably another of my chauvinist attitudes." He turned away from her and strode on. Andy had to skip to catch up with him. She reached out to put a hand on his arm, but he jerked it away.

"Tif, please, I'm sorry. I was only hoping to understand what happened so I could understand you better."

He stopped at that and slowly faced her. The lines about his eyes and lips hardened. Even in the dark she saw the gelid glint as he ran his eyes coldly over her upturned features. Suddenly, he put his arms around her and drew her against his chest. She could hear the uneven thump of his heart and feel his breath stir her hair. "I suppose," he said on a deep sigh, "that we'll have to rake it over sooner or later. I can't really blame you for feeling as you do when you've only heard one side of the story."

"Is your side really so different?" She knew in her heart that it was. Everything she'd learned of him thus far had been vastly different from her expectations. But she wanted very much to be convinced once and for all that he wasn't the unreasoning, tyrannical husband Carol had claimed he was.

"I guess you'll have to be the judge of that. Come on." He took her elbow and steered her to where they'd left their gear piled on the sandy ground. While she spread their mats and bags out, he collected two bowls of washing water. When he returned, they brushed their teeth and washed up, splashing water over one another playfully in the process. Finally, they sat side by side on the bags and opened a bottle of white wine that Tif pulled from his bag. Packed for, he told her, a special night.

He rested his arms on his kneecaps as he dangled the bottle between his knees. Andra didn't press him, sensing that he needed to tell his side in his own way. He did.

"I admit I resented Carol's career," he began finally, drawing on the wine between sentences, "but not for the reasons you suspect. I was proud of her accomplishments. She wasn't just good at what she did, she was better than most. She started out logging commercials at a local station and within three years was the assistant programmer. That's an impressive achievement for anyone."

He took a long swallow of the wine, a sweet liebfraumilch, then restlessly swung the bottle. "The problem was that in order to get so far so fast, Carol had to be committed to her work one hundred percent. She was. I resented her commitment. She cared far more for that damn station than she ever did for me."

"Maybe that's only how you perceived it," said Andy softly.

"No. Everyone else saw it, too. One day a friend of ours teased her, saying she should have married the camera and microphone instead of me." Tif studied his knuckles in the moonlight. "That's when it hit me. I was jealous of a goddamned TV station. If it had been another man, I could have handled it, but a program schedule—how the hell do you defeat that?"

The bitterness in his confession roused all Andy's earlier jealousies. She wanted to tell him she understood clearly—after all, to be jealous of a memory was even worse. Memories aren't even tangible. You can't fight an intangible. Suddenly, she wished she hadn't brought the subject up. What was the use? To remind herself that she was nothing but a substitute for Carol? She certainly didn't need reminding. The knowledge had been with her all day of every day of this trip.

She leaned forward and took the wine bottle from his hands. Setting it aside, Andy leaned closer still. A breath away from his lips, she deftly flicked her tongue over the fullness of his mouth. She placed her hands atop his knees, then let them drift slowly down to his thighs to the throbbing center of his desire. The audible change in his breathing told her she'd succeeded in diverting him—if not from thoughts of Carol, then at least from speaking of her.

With abrupt intensity Tif pulled her tightly into his arms, deepening the kiss, probing the moist inner warmth of her mouth. His hands sought the sweet secrets beneath her clothes, delving hungrily over each curve and hollow of her figure. As he fondled and caressed and tasted, Andy gave herself up to the delicious sensations he aroused. When they came together, their nakedness bathed in the magical moonlight, she promised herself not to think beyond the week they had left. She promised herself not to think.

Straight shafts of sunlight ricocheted over crystalline waterfalls dashing down the rocks of Elves' Chasm. It shone against the gold of Dennis's earring as the oarsman poised, then gracefully dove from a high ledge to the peaceful pool below.

"*Ex*—cell—ent," said Robin in admiration. That and "Oh, gross," seemed to comprise her entire vocabulary, but this time Andy agreed wholeheartedly with the teenager. The dive, the day, the chasm itself, were all excellent.

Elves' Chasm was a lush oasis hidden in the steep shade of the desertlike canyon. A spring-fed stream coursed into gloriously clear pools. Maidenhair fern and columbine, willows and helleborine orchids spread from the pools through the small groves bordering the cool grotto. An idyllic sense of peace permeated, blossoming with the flowers, humming with the birds, cascading with the waterfalls. No hike anywhere had ever been more amply rewarded, and the hikers now plundered the treasure they had found.

Andra sprawled on a narrow ledge, soaking up sunshine and drying her newly washed hair. Warblers sang in redbud trees, competing with the splash and tinkle of the waterfall, the laughter and merriment of the swimmers below. Eyes closed, she listened in appreciation, hoping this enchanted day would stretch on into infinity.

"Up with you, you lazy landlubber! You're worse than one of the rock lizards." Tif lifted her to her feet, ignoring her protests to rub his palm over her buttocks. "Ummm, I'm tempted to hide your jeans for the rest of the trip."

She flushed lightly. Her coral swimsuit was a rather daring one-piece, the sides completely cut away and the top and bottom joined together in front by a thin concave curve of material between breast and belly. Her back was bare, the string ties knotted at her nape. Not being very active athletically, Andy hadn't worn it much. Tif's reaction when she'd stepped from her jeans and shirt had thrilled her—the admiration in his eyes had darkened to a hunger that left her knees weak.

Pressing his body against hers, letting her know that his desire for her hadn't faded, Tif backed Andy to the rock's edge. Her own yearnings flared anew. In his tight black trunks he looked like a glowing, golden god, magnificently in shape and incredibly sexy. While her body melted in response to his, Andy still weakly resisted. "Please, Tif! I just washed my hair."

"So?"

"So I was letting it dry."

"It'll dry later. Hair as short as yours dries in no time."

A vision of Carol's long blond waves flashed in Andy's mind. By the time she thrust it away to object, "But—" Tif had gently pushed her over the edge. They fell together in a spray of warm water. Andra came up sputtering and choking, spitting water from her open mouth. Tif came up clinging to her and laughing.

She shoved water at him with the heel of her hand, then tried to escape before he retaliated. She failed. His hand circled her wrist, and he pulled her beneath the pool's surface. There, his arms and legs entrapped her, his mouth captured hers. Bubbles rose above them. If she were swimming in champagne, Andy was certain she couldn't possibly be more intoxicated. She thought Tif should be labeled, "Caution, Powerfully Potent Male. Take in Small Doses Only."

Later, drying together beneath the leaves of a box elder tree, she told him this. He shook his head, sprinkling her cheek with a vaporous mist from his damp hair. He propped up on an elbow and said seriously, "That makes me sound like a ladies' man. I'm not."

"No?" She raised her brows in teasing disbelief.

"No."

"You surprise me, Mr. Wilson, indeed you do."

"That's possibly because you don't know me, Ms. James. I've never been one to chase around. I'd rather have one woman for a dozen years than a dozen women for one."

Andy rolled onto her stomach to hide her face from him. She knew him enough to know which woman he'd rather have. The knowledge hurt.

He bent over her and lightly slid his fingertip down the length of her spine. She shivered. "What about you?" he drawled. "Are you the kind of woman who likes to flit from man to man, enjoying each new conquest?"

"That's an insulting question I shouldn't deign to answer, but—" She shrugged and his finger swirled downward. "In a word, no. I'm not the kind of woman who attracts men that way, for one thing, but even if I were, I've never had the time to invest in gathering conquests, as you put it. I've either been working toward becoming an attorney or working at being a damn good one."

He traced the coral curve of her suit from hip to hip. "I know you thought that I fought the divorce to get back at Carol, to make her suffer."

She twisted her head to look at him over her shoulder. He was intently following the movements of his finger. His eyelashes were lowered on his cheek, and she couldn't read his expression. "No, I—"

"It's not true," he cut in. His fingertip slipped beneath the slick material of her suit. "I fought it because I believe that marriage is a commitment. Carol wanted to solve our problems by getting rid of them, getting rid of me. I wanted to work them out together."

"Because you loved her," whispered Andy hoarsely.

"Because I felt committed to try," he corrected.

His hand worked its way beyond the edge of her suit. He kneaded the soft flesh, and she mewed with pleasure.

Leaning over her, nuzzling her nape with his breath, caressing her thighs with his, he murmured huskily, "Did you know the Wardices have been married thirty-four years? They got married before it became the rage to divorce the first time something went wrong."

"I . . . like them. . . ." she moaned. Her body was tingling. Her breath came in uneven gasps. She couldn't think. Why were they discussing the Wardices, for Pete's sake?

He turned her to face him. She stared at him through the veil of her half-closed lashes and saw him watching her pulse flutter in her throat. He lowered his head, and the soft thickness of his drying hair feathered her chin as he kissed the beat of her pulse. The beat accelerated. She thought she would faint with anticipation. Was that a warbler singing or her own heart?

"Why have you never married?" asked Tif, his voice slowed.

She ran her hands restlessly over his back before answering. "I never found anyone I could . . . care for . . . that way," she said at last. *I never found anyone like you.*

Tif cupped her breasts in his palms, gently rotating until her nipples thrust stiffly against the material. He sprinkled hurried kisses over her chin, her cheeks, her brow, before lowering to the ripe fullness of her pliant lips.

Andra gripped the lean bones of his hips, digging her fingers into the flesh beneath his trunks. She felt him harden against her. She heard his breath stagger, his heart thud.

He threw his legs over her, trapping her beneath his powerful length. Fumbling with the knot at the back of her neck, he continued to shower her with a heated storm of kisses. Realizing dimly that they couldn't progress much further in the open view of the chasm, Andy pushed feebly at his arms. They tightened about her.

"Love me, Andra," he groaned unsteadily.

"Here?" she queried on a ragged laugh.

An inscrutable expression crossed over his features, erasing the impassioned flush on the tawny skin. He lay tensely still for several seconds, then rolled from her. He cast an arm over his eyes and didn't speak until his breath was calmed.

"I guess that would be an eye-opener for some of our passengers," he said with a hint of humor.

"Especially Robin Wickes. I can hear her now: *Ex*—cell—ent!"

They both laughed. Tif sat up and hauled Andy upright, too. Gazing at her warmly, his gray eyes shining like polished pewter, he whispered, "That, my sweet, would be an understatement."

They slipped back into the water, continuing the enjoyable cycle of swimming and sunning, bathing and basking. Most of the day was whiled away at Elves' Chasm, but at length, knowing all good things must come to an end, the group began the long climb up the narrow, twisting slot leading back to the canyon. Progress from ledge to ledge, many without clear-cut handholds, was slow. They traversed the cliff single file, the oarsmen interspersed to give a helping hand, boosting and pulling and encouraging where necessary. Tif stayed by Andy, but when they came to one extremely thin strip of rock, a single voice shrieked above the rest, "I *cannot* crawl over that!"

With an apologetic grimace, Tif left Andy to reassure Nancy. He guided her across the strip, speaking to her in a soothing monotone all the way. Andy watched, admiring and wondering at his patience, then started to traverse the ledge herself. She was halfway across when she happened to glance down at the chasm some two hundred feet below. She glanced and her foot slipped all in the same instant.

She had no time to scream. Her foot twisted and she

spiraled forward. Colors flashed in a kaleidoscopic whirl. Buff, cinnamon, maroon, sunstruck silver rushed dizzily at her, then receded. Her arms flew out, and by some miracle she caught hold of a jagged edge of rock. She smacked against the cliff, striking her side and scraping her cheek. A grunt was knocked from her, then she lay motionless, dimly aware of shocked gasps and muted cries. Above the clanging of her heart, she heard Tif call out, asking if she could stand.

"I think so," she wheezed. She slowly, painfully, pulled herself up, skinning her bare elbows and knees on rough-cut rocks. But when she tried to step on her right foot, it buckled. She sank to her knees, unmindful of the cutting pain.

"Just stay there," ordered Tif. "Hold on."

He signaled, and after a breathless lifetime Mike came up on the ledge behind her while Tif appeared before her. Together, they managed to half-drag, half-push her the rest of the way. Once they reached the point where the ledge widened to a plateau, the entire group cheered. Andy looked from her grazed palms to her abrased elbows, past her cut knees and down to her swelling ankle. She summoned up a weak smile for the benefit of those around her, but she'd never wanted to indulge in a good cry more.

While the rest stumbled across the ledge, Tif stretched Andy prone and crouched on his heels to examine her ankle. He turned and prodded and poked it until she gasped, "Is this a test to see how much I can take?"

"I'm sorry. I need to determine just how badly you're injured. I don't think it's broken. It may be a pretty bad sprain."

Standing behind him, one of the boatmen rubbed his hand over his beard while eyeing Andra speculatively. "Should we radio for a rescue copter to take her out?"

"No!" Tif's fierce response sliced the group's babble like

a fine-honed ax. He sent one white-hot glare in Steve's direction, then returned his attention to Andy. He checked the side she'd rammed into the rock, cautiously feeling the bruised rib cage before again running his hands over her swollen ankle. "It's just a sprain," he muttered into the continuing silence.

"Won't be sure till she's X-rayed," said Steve laconically.

"Steve may be right," put in Mike. For once his cheery grin was missing. "Even if it's a sprain, how would she get around?"

Tif said nothing for a very long time. Andy's heart thumped so hard she thought it wouldn't matter if her ankle was broken or not. She was going to expire of a heart attack. The savage denial which had exploded from Tif had detonated an unbearable excitement within her. He cared! She knew that Steve and Mike were right. She knew that Tif knew it. His muscles were knotted tensely, his face set grimly as he squatted beside her. He knew, yet he didn't want to let her go. She thought she would pass out from the thrill of being wanted so much by him.

Finally, Tif pivoted on the balls of his feet and slowly straightened to stand before his boatmen. "I will take full responsibility. Unless Andy decides otherwise—" his voice grated harshly "—we'll not radio for a helicopter. Now, let's go, we still have a lot of river to run. Rick, stay with me."

It was the voice of command, and no one dared breathe any further argument. Held upright between Rick and Tif, Andy hobbled back to the rafts. The short hike was miserably painful, for despite all their care, both her injured side and ankle were bumped and thumped unendurably often. Her lips were white, her eyes glazed, by the time they finished packing and wrapping her ankle, doctoring her scrapes, and helping her into her jeans and shirt. When she was propped into the raft beside Karla, Andy was actually considering asking for the helicopter.

She longed to be swaddled in clean, crisp linens on a soft bed. She yearned for the soothing comfort of a sheer nightdress and fuzzy slippers. She wanted to watch a silly sitcom in air-conditioned ease. She wasn't cut out for the adventuresome life. What had ever made her think she was? If she'd ever needed proof to the contrary, the beige bulge around her ankle was it. She didn't want to suffer the wilderness one day more!

All such thought vanished when they beached. Tif bent, lifted her into his arms, and carried her away from the camp. Even separated by the bulk of two life jackets, she could feel the rapidly increasing hammering of his heart. Gently, he placed her on the flat, sun-warmed surface of a secluded boulder, then leaned with arms braced on either side of her.

"Do you want to leave?" he asked without preamble.

She heard the struggle to keep his tones even. She licked her lips. They were dry. Her mouth was dry. "Do you want me to?" she croaked.

"The rest of the journey wouldn't be easy for you. Tomorrow we make a two-day camp, primarily for a day's hike up Tapeats Canyon. So either you miss out on the fun or you participate in pain. And I could be wrong. Your ankle could be fractured; a bone could be cracked."

"You didn't answer my question."

The muscles in his arm stiffened. He looked down at the elastic bandage covering her ankle. "No," he said in a violent undertone. "No, damn it, I don't want you to leave. Not unless you're so miserable you have to go."

With that, all her misery, her aches, her desire for the comforts of civilization, simply disappeared. She gripped his head between her hands and forced him to look at her. "You'd have to break every limb I own to get me to go," she declared hoarsely.

His arms wrapped around her in a crushing clinch. She ignored the abuse to the tender bruise on her side and fully returned his passionate embrace. He stripped off his leather gloves, flinging them into the distance, then wove his fingers feverishly through her hair. With a low, guttural groan, he did as he'd once said he wished to do and kissed her senseless. Gone were the gently loving, playful kisses of teasing tongue and nibbling teeth. His mouth engulfed hers in a turbulent seeking of souls. He sought—and won—possession.

Andra surrendered willingly.

His hands moved with impatient intensity over her cheeks, her jaw, her throat. When he attempted to caress her breasts, however, he encountered a barrier of orange canvas. He cursed. Instantaneously, in unison, they broke apart laughing.

"I thought you boatmen were like boy scouts and always prepared," chided Andy, her eyes twinkling. Her lines of pain had been totally erased, and her features sparkled with merriment.

"Believe me, I am prepared," he returned on a husky whisper. He cupped her hand in his and guided it to the center of his cutoffs. "For you, always."

She sucked in her breath at the passionate rasp of his voice, the firm swell beneath her palm, the charcoal haze in his eyes. "Don't you think . . . we'd better . . . get back?" she said unevenly.

He reluctantly agreed and after one last tantalizing kiss carried her back to the main camp. Divesting her of her life jacket, he positioned her where she might feel a part of the preparations and departed to help unpack the remaining gear.

Over a dinner of huge grilled hamburgers, the story of Andy's fall was told and retold, each detail analyzed from a differing perspective. She was surprised at the attitude of her fellow campers. Sometime during the evening, each one had paused to inquire how she felt, ask if she needed anything, pat her on the back in an effort to cheer her. She remembered how left out she'd felt at the beginning of the trip and wondered how she had failed for so long to share the beauty of the camaraderie in this close-knit company.

When night stole over them in a cloak of pinks and purples, Mike pulled out his recorder and serenaded the sunset. Flames of melted gold burned brightly against the metal of the firebox. A stilled wistfulness seemed to descend with the darkness. Mike roused them by playing a lively tune. With a wry grin he told them he'd written it for Andy. It was called, he said, "Ode to a Gimp."

"It should be called, 'Ode to a Klutz,' " corrected Rick.

"Or to a walking demolition derby," suggested Tif.

"But she's not walking anymore," objected Mike. He ran a considering fingertip down the end of his mustache. "A limping demolition derby doesn't quite have the same impact."

"She's already had her impact," pointed out Howard Jacobson.

"Several times," his wife added. She directed a loving smile at her husband; Andy realized that somewhere in the spell of Elves Chasm the Jacobsons had resolved their differences. At least for now.

Someone questioned this banter, and to Andy's mortification the tale of her earlier misadventures with cactus and dehydration were related to those who'd joined the rafters the day before. But though she was the target of the evening's humor, it was all good-natured, with a strong foundation of affectionate concern. Andy was deeply touched. Since her circle of friends had diminished over the years, she'd forgotten how heartwarming such companionable concern, how uplifting such affectionate amusement, could be. When Tif at last hauled her into his arms and carried her to their sleeping rolls, her eyes were blurred with tears.

Try as she might, Andra could not keep them from spilling over. The scrape on her cheek glistened beneath the teardrop's caress. Tif caught sight of the crystalline track and his hold constricted.

"My god! Are you hurting? Where? Andy!"

She flinched as his arm compressed against her sore ribs. He bent and eased her into the sand. As he started to turn away, she cried, "Wait! Where are you going?"

"To radio for a helicopter," he replied through tight lips.

"But there's no need!"

"No need?" he echoed, incredulous. "Andy, I can't let you suffer like this. Darling, you have to be properly cared for."

She was so dazed by the throbbing ardor of his voice as he called her darling that she actually let him get three long strides away before calling out to him. "Tif! Come back! I'm fine, really!"

He paused, hesitating, then came back to kneel beside her. "God knows I don't want you to go, but you have to. I admire your courage, Andy, but I'm not letting you go on in this pain. You can't hide the truth. Your tears, your flinching, tell me that I've got to summon that copter."

Normally, Andy would have tried to talk to him rationally, explaining and convincing with all the expertise of her years of training. But the emotions of the day—the love and laughter, the fright and the discomfort, the excitement and the passion—they all tumbled together and came charging out in one hysterical hoot of laughter.

She stared into his concerned eyes and howled. She buried her head in her hands and laughed until her sore side became numb. Tears streamed down her face and through her fingers. Every so often, she'd raise her head, sputter, "My . . . my *courage!*" and succumb to a fresh gale. When she could laugh no more, she hiccupped.

After the first stunned minute, Tif got up and busied

himself with spreading out their bags. When he had their bed made, he carried Andy to it and removed her clothing piece by piece from her shaking, but nonresistant form. He pulled his gray T-shirt over her hiccupping head, then handed her a canteen of water. At his command to drink, she did so. Her hiccups and her hysteria faded away together. When she'd swallowed several healthy drafts, she gave it back and eyed him calmly, if somewhat guiltily.

"You flinched," he said in accusatory tones.

"What else could I do when you squeezed so tightly here?" she asked, pointing to her bruised side. She smiled. He frowned.

"You were crying with pain."

"I was crying from . . . emotion. I felt so happy, so engulfed in everyone's concern. It really touched me." She spoke in a quick, short burst, somewhat embarrassed by her feelings. With unaccustomed shyness, she added, "I think I understand why you love to do this. It isn't just the beauty of the canyon or the thrill of the river. It's the ability to share such fellowship with others, isn't it? Here, everything's back to the basics. Here, there's an exchange of the brotherly love so lacking out there."

She waved toward the rim. Her hand was caught in midair by his. In a gesture which honored her, he kissed the back of it. His lips lingered there, his breath caressing her skin. Andra's heart stopped. She stared at the pearlescent glimmer of his hair, and her entire being washed over with love. A love that wanted to give and share and possess for all time. Most of all she longed to entrap this moment forever.

But he raised his head, and the moment slipped away.

CHAPTER NINE

"Do you think life out there still exists?" Andy asked Tif, then sputtered as he shoved her head down in the cool rushing water of Tapeats Creek.

"Do you care?" he queried when he lifted her head to douse it with lathers of shampoo.

"If you do that again, Wilson, so help me, I'll—I'll—"

He ceased working soap into her hair and twisted down to face her. "You'll what?" he inquired with interest.

"I'll make you sorry!" she finished lamely.

"So? You've done that from the day I met you." He resumed washing her hair, frothing the shampoo in a swirling motion over her scalp.

Her wince was hidden from him. By the time he finished rinsing her hair and began whisking a towel over the wet locks, she'd schooled her face into a cheery display. Not for the world would she let him see that she'd been hurt by his quip. She knew she really shouldn't feel hurt; whatever had occurred between them in the past, he definitely wasn't sorry to be with her now. He'd practically chased the rest of the group away this morning, leaving the two of them in camp alone.

It was the second day they'd camped by the creek. Despite her aches and bruises, despite her limited mobility, despite her peeled nose and cracked nails, despite her inner uncertainties, Andra had never been happier. As soon as Tif had sent the merry adventurers on their hike up Tapeats Canyon, he'd flung off his clothes, then hers. As she shrieked in protest, he'd tossed her into the creek amid the watercress and trout, then leaped in beside her. They'd swum, then bathed, then he'd washed her hair.

They traded places on the creekbed, and she began rubbing shampoo into the thickness of his beautiful blond hair. A rivulet of soap-laden water raced down her arm, and her momentary dejection passed. This, now, here, was all that mattered.

"You know, the Russians could've captured Washington," she mused, flicking lather in all directions as she waved a hand in emphasis. "Revolution could be in the streets. The bomb could've gone off. How would we know?"

"I repeat, do you care?"

"Well . . . we're pretty isolated. It seems forever since I looked at a newspaper or heard a news bulletin. It makes me feel . . . odd . . . vulnerable."

"It makes me feel grateful."

"Grateful?" She stopped washing to stare at him. "Grateful?"

He pushed her hands away and quickly rinsed all the shampoo from his hair. When he was done, he sat up and shook like a dog coming out of a bath. A fine spray splattered over Andy until she forced a towel into his hands. "Yeah," he said as he fluffed his hair. "I'm grateful that there's still somewhere in the world where you truly can get away from it all. Away from the noise and the congestion and especially from the never-ending stream of news. I could live without most of the news."

She was shocked and looked it. "But wouldn't you want to know—really—if the world had been blown up?"

"Really?" He shrugged. "I suppose so. But for a few weeks at a stretch it's wonderful to get away from all the worry, to not hear the daily murder reports, politician's rhetoric, or dismal economic assessments. But if the world *has* been blown up," he said decisively as he tossed the towel aside, "we have a duty to perform."

As he reached out for her, the puzzled crease in Andy's brow appeared. "What duty?"

He traced the dark aureole of her breast with his fingertip. Her nipple hardened, a round, pink turret of firm response to his touch. He bent forward to dart his tongue over its grainy texture, and a sigh of pleasure escaped her. Abruptly, he lifted her and her legs automatically wrapped around his hips. He carried her into the creek, kissing her throat, her jaw, her ear, as he did so. There, he finally replied on a slurred rasp, "We have a duty, my dear, to repopulate the world."

"But—"

"I won't hurt you, darling, I swear it," he murmured, misunderstanding her objection.

Because of her injuries they'd not made love the past two nights. But they'd exchanged enough tantalizing caresses and teasing kisses to make Andy throb with desire. Stopping him was the last thing on her mind. She tightened the circle of her legs about his musculature, wreathed her arms around his neck, and gave her lips up to the fervor of his.

He nibbled on her lower lip while massaging her shoulders, then her arms, her breasts, belly, hips. The soft, cool kneading of her flesh reduced her to a quiver of pulsating need. The water gave her body a magically smooth patina, and his hands seemed to float over her contours. Beneath her fingertips, he felt equally smooth. Wet, warm, wonderful.

"We aren't going to repopulate anything this way," she said on a throaty laugh.

"Is that a dare?"

She inexpertly batted her eyelashes at him while wiggling her hips within his hold. "Are you a betting man?"

He chuckled hoarsely. "You're on!"

Cupping her bottom in his hands, he waded through the water to a low sand bar. He settled her with her shoulders propped on the ground while the rest of her remained submerged. He lay atop her and began sliding his hands from her hips to the soft undersides of her breasts. His long, smooth strokes gently sloshed water over them and quickly carried Andra into a dizzying whirlpool of need.

Tremors shook her entire body. "I still win," she panted into his ear. "This isn't doing the world any good . . . I'm on the—"

"The hell with the world," he muttered. Pressing his weight against her, he took her breast lovingly in his mouth.

She gripped his back, which was shiny with exertion. She could feel his own taut excitement and incited him further with rippling kisses and spiraling caresses. In return he kissed and touched and tantalized until she cried out for him to love her.

Slowly, carefully, he filled her. The water slapped against them in a rhythmic gurgle, imitating his even pumping. The creek was cool, but their bodies burned together in a silken, swaying cadence. Beneath the surface of the water their legs entwined, flowing in a slick undulation. As his control began to evaporate, his measured thrusts transformed to spearing demands. Water splashed wildly. Sunshine reflected miniature rainbows in the mist. A breeze ruffled over them, stirring the lingering scent of soap. Sand dug unnoticed into Andy's back.

She was aware only of Tif. Of the sand she felt clinging to his back, of the sun-heated warmth of his shoulders, of the tension of his arms and the ripple of his buttocks as he moved. For her the world had indeed ceased to exist. For her there was only Tif. Only Tif loving her.

She arched toward him, toward completion.

When the tumult came, he lifted his head and cried out her name. At that moment Andra felt herself fuse with him. She was his, utterly.

As their bodies relaxed, Tif leaned to bestow upon her the lightest of kisses. "Thank you," he groaned against the fullness of her lips.

Andra thought nothing had ever been, could ever be more perfect.

The morning was flawless. The creek sparkled. The sun shone. The sky shimmered. It was their personal paradise, and they reveled in it. It was as if they shared a mutual thirst which could not be quenched. They loved and played, then loved again.

Eventually, they donned their swimsuits with open cotton shirts thrown over them and prepared a lunch of cold cuts, cheese, lemonade, and beer. In the shade of a scrawny cottonwood, well away from the many barrel cactus scattered over the ground, Andy sat braced against their rolled-up bags, her legs stretched across Tif's lap, her ankle once again bandaged. She studied the bits of lemon clinging to the inside of her tin mug, then flicked at them with the tip of her tongue.

"Lucky mug," said Tif, directing a mock frown at the tin.

She looked up and their eyes met. Her breath caught. Surely, surely, that was something far stronger than mere physical attraction she saw glimmering in his!

Heartbeats later Tif tore his gaze away, and Andy gradually resumed breathing. That look, added to the passion of the morning, gave her renewed hope that their relationship would have a future. She remembered his fierce desire to keep her with him. She remembered and her hope grew. He would not let her leave without a promise to see her in Kansas City.

Biting into a hunk of sharp cheddar, he interrupted her musings to ask, "Have you come any closer to finding yourself the last few days?"

She had. She'd found herself, here, with Tif. But could she chance telling him that? She couldn't, not yet. Finding an absorbing interest in her lemonade, she replied without looking at him, "Oh, I don't know. I'm not worrying about it. I'll worry about it when I get back home."

Home. That seemed like a remote dream, a concept so distant it no longer held any meaning for her. This was home. Didn't they say home was where the heart was?

Wanting to distract herself, she inquired briskly, "Tell me, what do you do when you're not risking your life on the rapids? I mean, are you into all kinds of sports?"

He grinned. "Is that a note of caution I detect in your voice? No, I'm not much of a sportsman. I like to keep fit, but I'm not fanatic. In the winter I like to ski. Have you skied?" She shook her head, and his grin broadened. "Skiing has a lot of the same excitement as rafting. It requires the same constant maneuvering." He looked meaningfully at the Ace bandage wrapped around her ankle. "I'm not sure you'd be cut out for it, though."

"And what do you mean by that?"

"Isn't the evidence obvious?" He tickled the foot lying in his lap, and she squealed, choking on her drink.

"Nurses are supposed to comfort, not torment," she said indignantly. After a brief silence, she suddenly queried, "Did Carol ski?"

Now, damn! Why had she asked that?

Tif didn't seemed bothered by her question. "Carol? Are you kidding? She made no attempt to share my interests."

"Did you attempt to share hers?"

Darn you, James, couldn't you just drop it?

He took a long pull at his beer, then crushed the can in his hand. "She only had one interest. Her job."

There it was. The bitterness. Andy nibbled on her lip, angry with herself for bringing Carol into the conversation. Why had she? Because, like Tif, she now had a compulsion to know about Carol. To know how and why he loved her. To know, perhaps, if she herself had a chance to gain that love.

They finished eating in silence. At meal's end, Tif cleared everything away, then spread one of the tarps over the sand. He fished around in an ammo can until he came up triumphantly with a well-worn pack of cards. Over a game of gin rummy, he talked to her about his life, his childhood in rural Missouri, his current position on the faculty of UMKC. In a few adroit questions he'd elicited the facts that though she loved her family, she wasn't particularly close to them, and that her upbringing had been liberal and independent.

"It wasn't that my folks didn't care. They just expected me to make my own decisions, to stand on my own. Mother told me that if you never leaned on someone else, you wouldn't fall over if the support was removed." The crease in Andy's brow puckered. She lay her hand on the tarp. "Rummy."

"Damn. Let's make it three out of four." He dealt out the next hand. "Standing on your own's great, but did they ever teach you about standing beside someone?"

"I suppose, but I got too wrapped up in school, then my work, to ever put it to the test." She was studying her hand, but she could feel his renewed tension. She made a silent vow to bite her tongue off at the earliest opportunity and turned the conversation to a neutral discussion of the last movie she'd been to.

She'd beaten him four games out of five by the time the first of the hikers returned to camp. Foremost among them was Rick. He immediately came up to tousle Andy's hair. "How ya doin', Gimp?"

Since the night of the accident this had become her universal nickname. She smiled and gestured for him to sit on the tarp. "Fine. How was the canyon?"

"You wouldn't believe it! We hiked up to a tributary named Thunder River. God, it's a paradise!" He missed the tender glance his two listeners exchanged. "A lush hanging garden amid cascading springs as clear as crystal and limestone caverns that take your breath away. I took over a roll of pictures there alone. And I got a great shot of a pink rattler."

Andy grimaced. "Great."

"Hey, it is! Pink rattlers aren't found anywhere else in the world. I figure if I get my film to the developer the day after we get back home, this time next week I'll be showing you what you missed!"

This time next week . . .

Andra busied herself with gathering up the cards sprinkled over the tarp. Only four more days with Tif. How had ten days gone by so quickly? She longed to reach out and capture the sun, to hold it still in the sky and stop time from proceeding.

Tif rose and strode off toward the people who were straggling into camp. She watched him with a greedy desperation, like a condemned man watching the smoke spiral from his last cigarette. His long, lithe body moved with a natural grace that made her stomach flip. His hair trapped the sunlight, keeping some of it to whiten the blondness of it.

The sight both pleased and pained her. How could something feel so exhilarating and so excruciating at the same time? Sighing, Andy forced herself to shift her gaze. She saw Karla strolling in, her long, dark hair swaying vivaciously. She waved and the brunette waved back, then came directly toward her.

"Hi. You want to join the line of hikers at the john?"

Karla hoisted Andy upright, then provided a shoulder for her to lean on. With a slow, awkward gait, they traversed the sand, heading upriver. Andy glanced sidelong at her human crutch. "Did you have a good time? Rick was tremendously impressed with the hike."

"Rick's impressed with everything."

"True," she agreed with a laugh, then added provocatively, "but especially with you."

Karla had a laugh that was like the music on a carousel, enticing, infectious. Her laughter rang out now, and heads turned in their direction. "With any female over fourteen and under ninety, I think."

"But more so with you," insisted Andy.

"Maybe, maybe not."

"But—but don't you *care*?"

Karla halted to look at her. "What do you mean?"

"Doesn't it bother you to think that in four days you may never hear from him again?"

A knowing light flashed through Karla's blue eyes. Putting her arm around Andy and moving on, she replied, "What good would it do me to be bothered? What will happen, will happen. Sure I care about Rick, and if something develops out of what we've known here, that's terrific. But if nothing does, it's okay, too. At least we shared something special here, and that can never be taken away from us. By knowing Rick, I've grown a little, changed a little."

They stopped at a cluster of scraggly mesquite trees. A number of women were ahead of them, so Karla held back and continued quietly, "Look, Andy, I can't waste time worrying about a future I can't see. I might die tomorrow, so I intend to enjoy today. To the hilt. That means enjoying being with Rick while I'm with Rick. When I'm not with Rick, then I'll deal with that."

These were verbalizations of many of Andra's own reflections. The problem was, while Karla really believed what she said and appeared to live by it, Andy was incapable of it. Looking to the future, worrying over what was to come, was part of her nature. Caring whether or not Tif would promise to see her back in Kansas City was a throbbing ache she couldn't relieve by any magical rationalizations.

But later, when everyone was back in camp and coils of smoke furled around the fire while a soft buzz of voices hummed, Andy's fears were forgotten in her contentment. Beneath the rising moon Steve cast for trout in the creek while Karla splashed merrily about with Rick and Dennis. A bit further downstream several women were washing their hair. To her right Robin and the girl with all the leg were playing a game of hangman with paper and pen borrowed from the California architect. To her left the Wardices and the Jacobsons were playing a rousing game of canasta. Others were scattered about, drinking, talking, dozing. Andra looked around her, feeling a resurgence of the companionship she'd felt two nights before.

Karla's right, she thought. Live for the moment.

Her gaze caught hold of the southern dentist. Her anger with him fell away. What right did she have to judge his actions? She smiled at him. The dentist smiled back and held up a piece of wood he'd been whittling. To Andy it looked like a lump of kindling, but she smiled harder and nodded her head encouragingly.

Over the next two days her mood continued to lift. Her days burst with beauty heightened by the sharing of it with friends. Through tranquil waters and treacherous rapids, Andra's appreciation of the awesome world around her expanded.

She was struck anew with the brilliant blending of colors on the castled cliffs, at the majestic splendor of shadow conflicting with sunlight on the canyon walls. She marveled over the drama of each golden sunrise, the spectacle of each radiant sunset, the sweet ecstasy of starlight over the ragged rim. She even discovered an appreciation of the sight of a scorpion scuttling over the sand, feeling more surprise at its straw color and small size than terror.

And always, there were the unexpected wonders of the river.

At Deer Creek a magnificent waterfall leaped down more than a hundred feet from a narrow cleft in bright red rock. Delicate fronds crept over the rocks, veiled in the misty spray. At Havasu Creek deep, clear, turquoise pools mirrored the surrounding red walls and bright green vegetation. Ferns and flowers bedecked cascading falls, as did cottonwoods, willows, hackberry trees. Swifts, swallows, warblers, hummingbirds, and other birds she couldn't identify flashed through the trees. The sky, the cliffs, the pools, provided a half day's playground of exceedingly scenic grandeur.

If her days dazzled her, Andra's nights captivated. Whether bathed in mystical moonlight or blanketed by stormy shadows, sprinkled with stars or circled by clouds, she exalted in the wondrous raptures of the nights.

On the night at Tapeats Creek, after all the playful loving in the daylight, Tif came to her tenderly beneath the glory of the moon. He worshiped her with his touch. Slow and gentle, he cherished her. It was as if only her pleasure mattered to him, almost as if only she mattered. On the following night, threatened by a violent sky and looming clouds, Tif's mood was solemn. For the first time he spoke as he possessed her, pausing to whisper how beautiful she was, how soft, how fragrant, how unique. Distant lightning trembled in the sky, and he proceeded toward the ultimate tempest.

Last night the air had hung heavy with anticipation. Like a shepherd with his flock Tif gathered everyone before him and once again reviewed safety procedures. He stressed what to do if the raft should flip over and how important it was not to panic. The worst of the rapids lay ahead—the savage, the perilous, the awesome, Lava Falls—and the entire camp pulsated with tension. Tif followed his speech with a conference with his crew. Andra, now able to limp about unaided, retired to their sleeping bags to await him.

She rolled out their bed, washed, slid into the T-shirt that had been her nightgown for nearly two weeks, and lay down. For a while she counted the spangle of stars above her, but eventually she could not ignore the wave of regret cresting within her. She would be leaving the day after tomorrow, and Tif hadn't yet said anything to her about a future beyond that. If he wanted to continue their relationship once he returned to Kansas City, he'd given her no indication of it. She closed her eyes to shut out the pain of her fear.

When she opened them, he was beside her. Had her mental incantation of love caused him to materialize? She started to welcome him with a smile, but the lift of her lips drooped as he lay next to her. Forbidding lines rigidly masked his face. In the darkness his usually warm gaze appeared cold, blank. Abruptly, wordlessly, he reached for her. He was like a conqueror fiercely commanding her surrender, taking her aggressively with hot, piercing thrusts. Once, when he knocked against her bruised side and she yelped, he paused, shifted, then drove on. Afterwards, sensing his need for silence, she stifled her need to question him. He held her clamped tightly against him through the night.

Now, at dawn, Andra lay awake and wondering. She wondered just what, if anything, she meant to Tif. The sticky heat of his body radiated against her. The steady, slow rhythm of his breath drifted over her ear. The regular thump of his heart knocked at her side. They were two people who had melted into one but were now two again.

Her attempts to reassure herself that he must feel for

her what she felt for him failed miserably. Not once on this trip had he spoken of love.

She did not expect his love. And yet she hoped . . .

Wrapped within his arms, she lay remembering each special moment they'd shared together. Surely he felt it too. Surely he meant to see her again. With each memory her hope grew. When he stirred, slowly wakening, she greeted him with a smile radiant with love.

"And you call me lazy," she said in low, caressing tones. "I thought you intended to sleep the day away."

Still drowsy, ruffled, and heavy-lidded, he stared at her until her heart began to pound. Whatever he felt, she loved him. She loved him and she needed to tell him so. She opened her mouth and took a breath of courage.

In a single, swift motion, he straddled her and took advantage of her parted lips. His tongue probed the sweet moistness of her mouth, his hands roamed restlessly over the round fullness of her thighs, hips, breasts. As suddenly as he'd captured her, he freed her, then further stunned her by asking tonelessly, "Did I hurt you last night?"

Mutely, unable to gather her scattered wits, she shook her head.

"Your side?"

Again, she signaled a denial.

He sighed, then let her go. "I hope I didn't hurt you. I would never want to hurt you." He sat up, moving away from her. She had to strain to hear him add, "You're much too . . . nice. I'm sorry."

He dressed and strode away, leaving Andy in a daze. *Nice?* That was something one said to a mild acquaintance or a friend, but not, definitely not, to anyone special. Her heart sank. With a dismal sort of gratitude that he'd stopped her from foolishly declaring her own love, she got up. She dressed, wishing she had makeup to hide behind, and hobbled toward the upriver facility. She would have to rely on playacting to keep from showing her true emotions.

Fortunately, her deceptive skills weren't put to much of a test. Everyone else was far too swept up in the prospect of taking on Lava Falls to notice how tightly strained her smiles were. The cleanup after breakfast was unusually silent. Only the oarsmen continued to talk and joke, but their voices rang jarringly, and their banter was sharply edged.

Caught up in her inner turmoil, Andra had no room to fear the coming battle with Lava Falls. Successfully retreating from thinking at all, she felt like a sleepwalker as she climbed into the raft, sharing it as she had on the very first run with Karla, Rick, and Brent. As on that first meeting with the Colorado, she tried to focus on everything except the powerfully working muscles of the oarsman in front of her.

Fleecy clouds skimmed across the azure sky above. At this point the walls of the canyon rose higher, sheerer, more intimidating than before. Along the river varieties of cactus and stunted mesquite squatted beneath the cliffs. Splinters of sunlight rebounded from river to rock and back again. The morning was brilliant, but Andra viewed it through dulled eyes.

At lunch the mood was one of frantic merriment. The laughter was hearty and forced, the grins broad and false. The first evidence of lava flows could now be seen. Tif, sitting cross-legged beside Andy, his hand resting on her knee, quietly quoted the leader of the first expedition through the canyon over a hundred years before.

"John Wesley Powell described it as a conflict of water and fire, imagining a river of molten rock running down into a river of melted snow. 'What a seething and boiling of the waters,' he said. 'What clouds of steam rolled into the heavens!' "

For a long moment no one so much as breathed. A

hushed stillness emphasized the reverence of the moment. Tif looked around, pausing infinitesimally on each face turned to his.

"The waters at Lava Falls still seethe. It's got a rating above 10, which, as you know, is not recommended. It's dangerous, it's savage. It's the most savage run of white water in North America. In two hundred yards Lava Falls drops thirty-seven feet, all of them raging." Again, Tif gazed steadily at each of his passengers. "Those of you who don't choose to risk it will climb over the rocks and be picked up on the other side. Those who want to ride through will be welcome. But no one has to prove anything to anyone. No one has to go through it. All right?"

Dumbly, in unison, twenty heads nodded. Unexpectedly, Tif flashed a dazzling smile over them all. "Then let's go!"

As he stood, he took Andy's hand and hauled her to her feet. His lips grazed her cheek, surprising her. Since they'd pulled ashore, he'd been the tender, caring Tif she'd come to love. It disturbed her even as it elated her. His mood swings were unaccountable, incomprehensible. But with the tingle of his brief kiss lingering on her skin, she forgot her disquiet and practically skipped, sore ankle and all, to the raft.

Some of her glowing excitement dimmed in the muted, sullen boom crackling ahead. A tremendous slab of black basalt, shaped like a gigantic tombstone, loomed in the midst of the river.

"Vulcan's Anvil," said Rick. His voice rang ominously. Andra instantly decided to buy him a muzzle for Christmas.

The rafts heaved to shore. Standing together in a small knot on the brink of Lava Falls, all eyes focused on the water violently battering the rocks below them. It was a furious cauldron of leaping, dropping, foaming waters. It was both a terrifying and a thrilling sight.

Andy shuddered, thankful she wouldn't be going through it.

"If there's anyone who says he or she's not afraid of Lava Falls, we don't want 'em in the rafts," shouted Tif above the tumult.

No one moved.

"Those of you who want to run it, gather here. We'd appreciate the encouragement of the rest."

For another tension-racked moment, no one moved. Then slowly, singly, people began to walk away. Andra took a half step, but was abruptly stopped by a firm clasp on her arm.

"You're coming with me," said Tif.

Her eyes widened. She tried vainly to pull her arm free. "Uh-uh. No way," she denied, hoping she sounded as implacably determined as he looked.

"And how do you propose to get over the rocks? Fly?" He shook her arm a little and exhibited his teeth in what she thought resembled a death leer. "You sure as hell aren't going to climb over them."

"But—but I'm sure I can—" she stammered.

"Like hell you can. You can barely manage to limp around on a flat beach. Some of those boulders are more treacherous than the water. If you should slip, you could easily break your already weakened ankle. You're coming with me and that's that."

Recognizing that merciless tone, Andra realized it would be useless to plead. The man had no pity, no understanding, no heart! He wanted to revenge himself upon her. He wanted—

Leaning down, he pressed his lips upon the sensitive spot behind her ear, then promised, "Don't worry, sweet. I wouldn't let anything happen to you."

She ceased fighting his hold. He could talk the sting out of the scorpions, she thought resentfully. She glared at him but remained passively at his side.

Most of the passengers elected to portage around the rapids, but a few foolish souls stood waiting for the signal to return to the rafts. Karla and Rick, Robin and Brent—these did not surprise Andy, for they'd already exhibited an alarming lack of healthy fear. But she gaped at the sight of the Wardices, gray heads nodding a smiling duet at her. Larry Hartigan had also chosen to ride the rapids, resisting his sister's imploring whine not to be so stupid.

Back in the raft, Andy gripped the nylon strap and twisted her lips in a feeble attempt to smile. Her knuckles whitened. They pushed off beneath a glaring sun. Squinting, Andy saw Tif's gloved hands tighten on the oars. She wanted to squeeze her eyes shut, but perversely they flew open as he steered them into the initial surge of Lava Falls.

Her first muttered prayer was choked off as the raft plummeted down twenty tumultuous feet, then tossed back up a steep watery slope. From that moment on, they whirled in a high-speed blender of plunging, rocking, rabid river. Huge waves furiously flung the raft toward jutting barriers of lava, then miraculously hurled them out of harm's way. Once, the rubber was bent double, nearly throwing Andy into Tif's back before bucking back into shape. She was vaguely aware of the oars striking the air, of Tif straining to pull them onward. Finally, a series of unrestrained haystacks washed wildly over them.

Then it was calm.

A half minute and it was all over. Cheers from those on the rocks wafted over them. With quivering arms, Andy loosened her manacled grip on the gear strap and began to bail. Tif began whistling as he rowed toward the shore.

Thoroughly drenched, shaking from a mixture of relief and intense satisfaction, she stood beside Tif and watched the next raft come through the falls. "You took me through *that?*" asked Andy in disbelief as she observed the twisting and tossing of the rubber as it leapt up, then vanished beneath the curtain of frenetic foam.

"You loved it," he said with certainty.

"I hated it."

"It was the thrill of your life."

"I hated it," she stubbornly insisted.

He laughed. He was still laughing when the first of the rock-scramblers joined them on the edge of the beach. Had her ankle not been damaged, Andy would have kicked him. As it was, she threw up her chin and refused to acknowledge him as she watched the last three rafts test the fury of Lava Falls.

But she forgave him everything—last night, this morning, the rapids, everything—when he swooped her into his arms, shouting, "And now we celebrate!"

In front of them all, he kissed her with a ferocity to outdo anything Lava Falls had thrown at them.

CHAPTER TEN

Twilight's pink blush mantled a merry campsite. Boisterous voices vied with one another to retell the tale of the mighty run through Lava Falls. No one agreed precisely as to what had happened, but all agreed it had been stupendous. It had seemed nearly as exciting for those who had cheered from the shore as for those who had rafted through it. For everyone, it had been the highlight of the trip.

For everyone, that is, except Andy. For her the highlight had nothing to do with the rapids, the river, or even the canyon itself. It had to do with the moment she'd first given herself to Tif. Now that, she thought with a secretive half smile, had been a thrill!

An excess of beer and brandy were quaffed. Constraints disappeared in proportion to the quantity consumed. Dinner was an almost unnoticed affair of salad and slumgullion stew. Once the remnants of the meal were cleared away, the revelry began in earnest. The oarsmen led the festivities with rousing recitations of campside jokes. Dusk fled before a bursting red and gold sunset that flamed over the rocky turrets, and tall tales gave way to rowdy, off-key singing. Soon, the majority were dancing unsteadily to the wispy music of Mike's recorder.

Andy watched the more energetic celebrating from the safety of her perch on a rock sheltered by the starlike leaves of a white brittlebush. Tif had carefully positioned her there before vanishing to swing Robin through an impromptu polka. He'd returned to snatch a brief kiss, promising her more in a throaty tone that pulsed in her blood like wine. Then with a grin, he whisked away to hug Edna down a serpentine conga line. Sipping slowly at a can of beer, Andy shook her head in amusement at the staggering progress of the line.

The laughter, the music, the ever-present gurgle of the river, all resounded with the same joyous elation she felt. The colorful spectrum of this party mirrored the celebration of her heart. When had she ever been so happy?

Happiness sang through her veins. After coming through Lava Falls, Tif had made his feelings clear. That twirling kiss had been Andy's pot of gold at the end of the rainbow. He would speak to her tonight, she was certain of it. The foundation of their future together would be laid on this, the last night of her trip through the canyon.

Hearing a snuffling sob, Andy swiveled on her rock. Peering into the shadows behind her, she saw an indistinct plump face crumpled with tears. "Nancy?"

"It's so sad!" wailed the blonde.

"What is?" asked Andy in bewilderment.

"This! It's the end! It's been the best two weeks of my life and it's over!"

The best two weeks of her life? *Nancy?* Wide-eyed with skepticism, Andy struggled to offer what consolation she could. "It's not over, Nancy, not really, not if you don't want it to be. I mean, you'll always have the memories, after all."

"Memories! Ha! What good are memories?" Nancy demanded with a soggy sniff. Her keening lament continued, but her words were indistinguishable in the midst of her torrential weeping.

What good indeed?

Pushing that disquieting thought aside, Andy turned back to view the diminishing train of dancers. Most of the conga line had toppled. She gazed unseeing at the few stragglers while reflecting how unpredictable people were. The last person she'd have suspected of bemoaning the end of this trip was the one who'd complained about it every inch of the way. People were funny, all right. She shook her head.

"And why, madam, are you shaking your head at me?" Tif tilted toward her and grinned crookedly.

"I wasn't," she laughed, "but looking at you now, I think I should have been. Tif Wilson, I think you're drunk."

"As a skunk," he agreed happily.

"Aren't you supposed to be setting an example here?"

He raised an offended brow. "I thought I was."

"Well, then, shouldn't you give your passengers something better than drinking to think about?"

"Like what?"

Turning her face up to his, she parted her lips. "I'm sure you'll think of something," she said breathily.

He did.

With a fluid ease which belied his claim to drunkenness, he folded his arms about her. He took possession of her mouth slowly, nuzzling and nipping and tantalizing Andra to the point of madness before claiming her lips in a fierce, deep demand. She wiggled within his hold, inciting him to rub one hand over the round curve of her buttocks and the other over the swell of her breast. Her heartbeat skipped into the palm of his hand.

Before he set an example that could be termed outright shocking, Rick appeared to demand Tif settle an argument between two of the men. Reluctantly, he released Andy.

Breathing raggedly, he promised, "I'll be right back. To take care of unfinished business, so to speak."

"I have"— she kissed his chin —"a better idea. I'll wait for you at our bed."

"*On* our bed."

"*In* it, if you like."

"Oh, I like, I like." He laughed as he finally responded to Rick's insistent tug at his arm. He blew her a last kiss as he stepped away.

She followed his progress across the camp with her eyes. Despite a slight swaying, he had a walk that demanded attention. The powerful strength exuded in the supple stretch of his flexing muscles couldn't be ignored. He stopped before a knot of campers, and even from this distance Andy could see his effortless display of authority. How had she ever mistaken that aura of command for ruthless despotism?

With another shake of her head, this in self-reproach, she slid off her boulder and limped away in the opposite direction. She wanted to freshen up while Tif was busy; that way, she'd be ready for him by the time he was free. Nearing a feathery cluster of tamarisk, she heard a low rumble of voices before she saw the shaded outlines of two men.

"Well, we got through another expedition," said one, whom she recognized as Steve.

"Yeah. Another cruise of the love boats comes to an end."

Andy stopped, stood still. The second voice belonged to the fifth boatman, Clayton. He'd rarely spoken throughout the length of the journey, but it wasn't surprise at hearing him speak that held her immobile. It was Steve's knowing chuckle.

"Ah, yes," he was saying, "the love boats. No crew ever had it so good."

"Not to mention," Clayton pointed out with a leering laugh that curdled Andy's blood, "the H.O."

"Oh, no doubt about it. Head Oarsman Wilson hasn't done too badly this go-round."

"He always gets the pick of the crop," said Clayton, sounding disgruntled.

"Yeah, but ya gotta admit life in the ranks ain't so bad." They walked on, and the rest of Steve's speech was lost to her.

Andra couldn't move for several minutes. Her pulse pounded savagely in her veins, and her heart kicked viciously against her chest. She tried to pretend she didn't care what she'd heard. She tried to pretend it meant nothing. She failed.

Deep down, she'd known all along that when the trip was over, so, too, would be her fling with Tif Wilson. Another group would arrive at Lee's Ferry to be taken down the Colorado River. Another group filled with young, lovely women ready to fall in love under the moonlight, ready to share the sensuous delights of the canyon with Tif.

She'd known, she'd just heard confirmation, and still she refused to accept. Even yet, a flicker of hope fluttered within her. There was still time for Tif to prove he cared enough to make something more of their relationship than a mere river affair.

Stumbling on, Andra collected her bowl of water and hobbled back to her gear, sloshing most of the water onto sand which dried instantly in the night's heat. She managed to wash, brush her hair into some semblance of order, and change into a crinkled, but fresh, pair of white denim shorts and a poppy-red blouse with short, puffed sleeves. There was nothing to be done to improve her damaged nails or unsightly bandaged ankle, but she felt she looked as good as she possibly could under the circumstances.

Thus prepared, she unrolled their bags and sat down to wait. And wait. Time was once again her enemy, only instead of moving too quickly, it now marched sluggishly. Where was he?

For once she actually heard Tif long before she saw him. A pleasant, lusty baritone belted out the lewd adventures of a gal named Sal and her man Dan. The song ended abruptly. His silhouette weaved into sight, his blond hair bobbing in and out of the shadows. Andy was reminded of another time he'd stood weaving drunkenly in the shadows, and a chill dread crept up her spine. She quivered as he drew near.

He stood looking down at where she sat, her legs stretched out on the sleeping bag. Darkness hid his expression but accentuated the taut immobility of his stance. Andy licked her lips but could not speak. Now that he was here, now that they were alone, her heart was leaping frantically. What should she say? Do? Would he yet speak?

"You look great in those shorts," he said at last, plopping down onto the bag beside her.

"My legs are too pale," she said inanely.

"Not too pale," he contradicted. He slid his hand slowly from the cuffed edge of her shorts to the curve of her calf, then back up. "Just right. Like moonlight."

Tingles scurried up her thighs. His swirling fingertips were a potent elixir, guaranteed to cure her ills. Doubts and fears began to ebb before the rising tide of her response to his touch. What could possibly be wrong when this felt so right?

"I can't be like moonlight," she murmured in protest. Spreading her fingers through the silvery web of his hair, she sighed, "All the moonlight has been caught in your hair."

His soft chuckle warmly caressed her neck. He pressed his lips on the hollow, then the arch, before progressing over her jawline to at last meet her eager lips. A myriad of sensations unbearably sweet assailed her, heightening her pleasure. The scent of sweat clinging to his skin, the moist tang of beer lingering on his tongue, the rasp of his legs rubbing against hers. Of all this and of none of this was she aware. One thing only did Andra really know. She knew she throbbed for Tif.

Abruptly Tif broke away. He sat up and yanked his shoes off, then his cutoffs. He glanced at where she lay motionless, drugged with passion. "If you don't want those clothes torn off, you'd better get rid of them now."

Had he thrown her bodily into the icy Colorado, he couldn't have destroyed her mood faster. Just like that he expected her to be ready for him. Snap the fingers and watch Andra roll over, was that it? She jerked upright. "What's the hurry? From the time you took to get here, I had the impression you weren't overly anxious."

"Sorry I took so long, babe, but"— he discarded the last of his clothes and stretched, a long, lean profile of alluring masculinity —"you know how it is. A boatman's work is never done."

"I'd have said you'd done more playing than working." She'd meant that to come out as a bit of teasing banter. It sounded more like acrid recrimination.

"So I stopped for an extra toast or two. What of it?"

None of this was progressing the way Andy thought it should. She'd envisioned this last night of theirs as being the highest peak, the most magical night in an enchanted string of nights. She'd imagined fierce kisses culminating in towering passion. Now, she silently twisted her hands together and wondered what had gone wrong so quickly.

"Hey, sweetheart," coaxed Tif, his voice husky, "let's not spoil tonight. We've got better things to do than argue." He leaned toward her and reached to take her in his arms.

Andy pulled back. Without meaning to, indeed, without wanting to, she blurted out, "What happens after tonight?"

His arms were still outstretched. Even in the deep shadows, she could see his puzzlement. "After tonight?" he repeated, sounding rather as if he were speaking a foreign language.

"Yes," she insisted. Prodded on by the ringing recollection of Clayton's leering laughter, she inched further away from him and demanded, "What's ahead for us in Kansas City?"

He stiffened, dropping his arms. "What's gotten into you?"

"Nothing's gotten into me. I just want to know where all this is leading."

She held her breath. The wind stirred the sand. Revelry's clamorous din echoed in the distance. The aroma of alcohol wafted from his breath. In those never-ending seconds of time, Andra realized what he would say before he spoke.

"It wouldn't be the same back in K.C.," he said finally, confirming her fears. "You go back to being Ms. James, superlawyer in starched linen suits. I go back to being Professor Wilson, instructor with two degrees and one divorce."

The rose-toned peak which crested in the distance blurred before her eyes. By sheer willpower she held back the tears. As if observing this entire phenomenon from afar, one part of herself congratulated her control. Another wondered how she could suffer such pain without release.

"That doesn't change what we've had," he argued.

"Perhaps not for you. For me, it changes everything."

"Damn it, Andy! It doesn't change the fact that I want you now, that you want me." He grabbed for her, but she darted away from his arms.

169

"Don't touch me! Just because you want me doesn't mean it's reciprocated!"

"What is this? Is this another game? You wanted me all right! You think I couldn't tell?"

"Don't flatter yourself!" she snapped.

She heard the sharp hiss of his breath and started to jump up. Tif lunged, yanking at her arms, pinning her into place. She struggled briefly, flailing and kicking uselessly. Realizing her inability to fight his strength, she sagged limply beneath him. The heat of his anger pulsed against her skin, his harsh breath grazed her cheek. Glaring at him from beneath her lashes, she saw a dark flush rise over his tanned skin.

"Let go of me," she demanded through clenched teeth.

His grip tightened, pinching her flesh. For a beat of her heart she thought he was going to force himself on her. But with an unexpected suddenness, he released her. She fell back, then quickly righted herself. Rubbing her arms, she refused to look at him as he rose to hastily and somewhat unsteadily dress.

A wall of barbed-wire tension separated them. Andra wanted to call back each of her words, to retrieve their last night together. She kept silent. Nothing could ever erase them. Nothing could take away the pain of her disillusionment.

Without another word he strode off toward the continuing carousal in the main camp. When she was quite certain he could no longer hear, she buried her head in the folds of her sleeping bag and wept. She had known all along that he couldn't, wouldn't, love her. She'd known his was a purely physical relationship. She'd known she was one of a long line of summer lovers. But knowing hadn't eased the heartbreak.

Sometime after midnight, when Andra had no more tears left to weep, the full, milk-white moon climbed above the rim of the cliffs. Shimmering light inched over the canyon until the muted pink spires of rock gleamed against the sapphire sky. When the globular moon hung high enough to clearly illuminate the shrubs and sand, rocks and river, she gave up the pretense of sleep.

Exhaustion or drink or both had at last claimed the merrymakers, and the camp lay in a golden glow of tranquillity. The bag beside her lay empty. She could only assume Tif had found another bed to share. Never having undressed, she now stood and began neatly rolling up his bag and mat, tying them together with an efficiency that would have stunned her fourteen days before.

As she quietly worked, she mentally reviewed the possibilities. She didn't think he'd stoop so low as to seduce Robin, and she'd seen the lady with the legs disappear with Mike earlier in the evening. The only other unattached female was Nancy. She heartily hoped Nancy whined through the whole performance. God, that would serve him right!

Finished, she curled up in her favorite thinking position, hugging her knees to her chest and resting her chin on the caps. She'd behaved foolishly, she saw that now, but regret was a waste of time. What she had to consider was her future. She'd come on this trip to straighten herself out, and in a way she had. She now realized that for years she'd stifled an important facet of her being. She'd channeled all her energies and emotions into her career. The part of her that needed to love, to share, to give and receive from another human, had been repressed, but not extinguished. This was, she believed, the source of her recent vague dissatisfaction with her life.

Unfortunately, now that she'd discovered what she wanted, Andra felt certain anyone other than Tif Wilson would fail to satisfy these needs of hers. She couldn't regret that, either. Loving him had been a brilliant achievement. After years of one-dimensional living, falling in love had made her whole, complete. No, she couldn't regret the last two weeks.

The notion of making the rounds of singles bars or dating services in an attempt to find someone else like Tif was both ludicrous and distasteful. Her only other option was to go on as she had before. To return to Kansas City and be the best damn junior attorney Colbern, Hanks had.

She was still coiled in a tight ball, planning her career and her lonely old age with a perverse sort of satisfaction, when the moon gave way to the coming of the sun. Dawn arrived gradually amid a haze of blues and golds that crept over the cliffs. With a sigh of gratitude for the long-awaited daybreak, Andy changed into jeans and her yellow terry cloth top, then repacked her duffel for the last time. She pulled out the gray T-shirt and held it, remembering the night he'd thrust her into it, the morning she'd yanked it off in front of him. Impulsively, she folded it back into her bag. He wouldn't miss one T-shirt. He probably didn't even remember giving it to her.

The rest of the camp roused slowly. Grunts and groans accompanied each stirring. Andra hauled her gear down to the main camp, then returned for Tif's. She made coffee and sat on a boulder staring at the muddy waters of the Colorado while drinking it. The one thing she didn't do was think. She'd finished with thought for the time being.

When she first saw Tif, he was walking toward the main camp with Dennis. From where she sat, she had the advantage of studying him unobserved. If he was hung over, he gave no sign, striding as purposefully, as gracefully, as ever. The attraction of the lithe motion of that trim, toned body struck her more powerfully than it had the first time she saw him. She longed to throw herself into his arms, to know again the taste and touch of him.

Dennis pointed to a pile of empty cans and said something. Tif's responding laughter carried on the wind to strike Andy like a slap. The breakup that was stabbing her with each splinter of her shattered heart clearly hadn't affected him in the least.

She moved with deliberation toward the metal grill where steam wisped from the coffeepot, timing her steps to intercept the two boatmen. She had no clear intent. She only knew she had to confront him.

They met. Tif stopped laughing. His gaze swept over her like a broom through a pile of dirt. Throughout the endless night she'd determined a thousand times she would not leave without telling him she was thankful for what he had given her, but it was obvious he wouldn't welcome so much as a glance from her. He stepped around her, blatantly ignoring her to pour two mugs of coffee. He did not speak to her, not then, not later, not even to acknowledge her care of his gear.

Amid the jovial preparations of the morning meal, Tif was conspicuously brusque, Andra conspicuously silent. It seemed to her that breakfast took years, and the cleanup following took decades. At last the rafts were loaded up for the short float down a calm stretch to the take-out point.

Here, as at Phantom Ranch, the party divided, most to continue on down the river to Lake Mead, the rest to travel by horse up a precarious, zigzag trail out of the canyon. The rafters lingered while the departing gear was loaded on small burros. To Andy, the process of farewells seemed interminable. Tif didn't come near her, which she thought was just as well. She had no doubt she'd have caused a ridiculous scene if he had.

"Are we going to wait here *all day?*" queried a petulant voice, and for once Andy found herself in complete agreement with Nancy.

Before she mounted her horse, Karla came up to give her a hug while prophesying that they'd be rafting together next year. Andy shook her head, knowing how impossible that dream was. "You take care, Karla. Remember, you're always welcome in K.C."

Karla swung her long, dark hair behind her shoulders and winked. "You might see me there sooner than you think."

Eventually, the horses began moving single file up the sheer precipice. Gripping the pommel of her saddle while praying beneath her breath, Andra looked back only once. At the sound of the last shouted good-byes, she swiveled and stared down at the river. She searched frantically among the waving group below, her heart hammering and her vision swaying in time with the measured pace of her mount.

He stood ramrod straight beside the beached rafts. He did not wave. Her last image of Tif was of bleached blond hair glinting in the sunlight.

A loose rock kicked under her horse's hoof to roll down the cliff. She turned her attention to the trail ahead and did not look back again.

She began to wonder if she'd survived Lava Falls only to lose her life on the cliff. Narrow and incredibly steep, the tortuous trail twisted sharply with several death-defying turns. In a way she was grateful. The continual terror kept her from thinking about Tif.

Once they reached the end of the trail, Andra looked down for the second time. She was surprised at her warped perception of the distance. From where she stood, it looked as though she could easily run down to the river and back again in a day. A layer of limestone formed a ring midway around the canyon wall, like a bathtub ring, which hadn't been visible from the river. The Colorado itself looked like a thin streak of silver winding aimlessly along. Of the rafts nothing could be seen.

"Hard to believe we were down there, isn't it?" Rick handed her a plastic cup of cool spring water, then raised his camera to snap several photos.

"Very," she agreed noncommittally. She slowly rotated as she drank the water, admiring the desolate grandeur surrounding them between sips. From here the brilliant variegation of reds and browns of the canyon were muted to a single rusty glow. Puffs of clouds lazed in the azure sky, occasionally screening the steady radiance of the sun. By the time she finished the water, the horses and burros were corralled, and their gear was reloaded into a trio of jeeps.

Lowering his camera, Rick grinned at her. "What did you think? Was I right? Were you thrilled?"

"I was thrilled, all right," she said with heavy self-sarcasm. "Right down to my socks."

Rick shot her a puzzled frown. He tugged at his sparse crop of hair and looked her up and down. "You okay? You've been drinking enough liquids, haven't you?"

She sighed. "I'm fine, Rick, really." *Except for my heart.*

"You're sure?"

"Trust me. If I look sick, it's an aftereffect of the morning's joyride. You could have warned me about that trail. I said my last prayers at least a dozen times on the way up. What's next on this agenda of horrors?"

As she'd hoped, this effectively turned Rick's thoughts. He chuckled, then drawled, "Well, we take a ride in those jeeps . . ."

"That sounds safe enough. Where to?"

"To the airfield."

"Oh, my god," said Andy. "I was wrong. Don't tell me any more. Ignorance is bliss."

"Hey, wait till we fly out over the canyon rim!" he exulted, ignoring her plea.

"Paisley," she bit out, "don't press your luck. Under the circumstances, I could get off with justifiable homicide."

His laughter followed her all the way to the jeep. Their driver was short and dark with skin as tough and crinkled as old rawhide. Shaded beneath the brim of a dusty Dodgers' baseball cap, his eyes were perpetually squinted, his crooked teeth bared in an endless grin. He drove with hair-raising speed, jarring his passengers to their back teeth as they bounced and jolted over rutted gravel roads that spiraled perilously upward, taking them further and further away from the canyon depths.

The airfield was a wide dirt runway. Two single-engine planes, painted white with wide blue stripes, stood at the far end, facing the edge of the canyon. Andy took one look and shut her eyes. Why hadn't she gone on to Lake Mead? Why hadn't she gotten off at Phantom Ranch? Why had she come here in the first place?

The takeoff was as terrifying as anything that had yet happened to her. She had no intention of looking at anything beyond her whitened knuckles. But when Robin yelled, "*Ex*—cellent!" she involuntarily glanced out the window. She glanced and then stared. The view was breathtaking. Only now was Andy able to fully perceive the majestic scale of the Grand Canyon. She couldn't tear her gaze away from the jagged tiers sculpted from the outer rim down to the serpentine twists of the Colorado which were just visible within the inner canyon so far below. It took an hour or less to reach Lee's Ferry, an hour or less to span the river it had taken them fourteen days to raft down.

Had it only been fourteen days? Just two weeks? It felt like a lifetime. As they came in for their landing, Andy craned her neck to gaze at the ribbon of river. She heard herself telling Nancy that she'd always have the memories. She'd been right. She'd always have her treasured memories. However painful, it had been worth it, this trip down the river of rapture.

CHAPTER ELEVEN

The sweeping staircase and Waterford chandelier looked like something out of *Gone With the Wind*. With the indifference of one long-accustomed to her surroundings, however, Andra mounted the plushly carpeted steps without casting a look either to the left or right. She did not need to see the wingback chairs, the flowered sofas, the delicately painted vases standing upon finely carved walnut side tables. She knew just how beautiful an image they presented. But four years familiarity had dulled her appreciation of the beauty of the entrance to Colbern, Hanks, Whitney, Sanders and Company.

As if by instinct she turned to the left and proceeded down a long corridor without lifting her eyes from the sheath of papers in her hand. A narrow line of concentration etched its way between her brows, only slightly marring her aura of efficient composure.

She automatically rounded another corner, knowing precisely how far she could walk before needing to raise her eyes. Her suede briefcase bumped rhythmically against her slate-blue skirt, adding an offbeat to the muffled staccato of her black pumps against the biscuit carpeting. At length she halted and abstractedly pushed open a door.

The elegant atmosphere which greeted one at the law firm descended by degrees from the palatial grandeur of Mitchell Colbern's enormous suite to the functional practicality of the squares accorded to the firm's most junior partners. Since she'd joined the firm, Andra had often been amused at the reactions of clients who, having been ushered from the opulent display at reception into the spartan efficiency of her office, gave way to astonishment, relief, or occasionally, resentment.

Today, however, she didn't pause for the least reflection on such matters. Dropping her briefcase on one of the two chairs positioned in the corners of the small cubicle, she shucked off her suit jacket, laying it over the edge of the desk. Moving to sink into the soft tan leather of her chair, she loosened the floppy, bone-white bow about her neck with one hand while lifting her phone with the other.

She cradled the receiver on her shoulder and flipped through a short stack of pink slip messages neatly centered atop her desk. Her nails glistened a deep cranberry that matched the polish of her lipstick. Though her nails weren't quite as long as they'd been two months ago, they were finely shaped and beautifully manicured, as flawless as her perfectly styled brown hair, as elegant as her silk suit.

"Jill? The Davies hearing has been rescheduled to the last week in October. Please note it on the docket calendar. Yes. The twenty-seventh. Thanks." She disconnected and began redialing in a single motion. She was just finishing her fourth call when her office door opened without ceremony.

Rick lounged in and settled himself comfortably in the nearest chair. He ignored Andy's unwelcoming grimace and graciously signaled for her to proceed with her call.

As she hung up, he began speaking, cutting off her opportunity to get rid of him.

"I'm telling you, Andy, that condo's a super deal, especially split with Karla and a friend of your choice."

"For the last time, Rick, no. I have no interest in going to Colorado to go skiing. I have no interest in skiing, period." The memory of a broad grin, a warm glance, and a deep voice explaining the excitement of skiing flashed painfully. She bent her head, as if intensely examining the next pink message slip, and hoped Rick wouldn't notice.

"Look, you liked rafting, didn't you? You'll love skiing," he persisted.

It requires the same constant maneuvering, rang in her ears, her heart.

"The way you've been working these last few weeks," he went on in his most persuasive tones, "you're going to need a break by the time January rolls around."

"I like my work."

"Sure, but twenty-five hours a day? You'll welcome the break, believe me. You'll have a great time. Out in the mountains with the thrill of the sport and good friends—what more could anyone ask for?"

"Read my lips, Paisley. *N. O.* Got it?" She smiled sweetly.

"Karla's really looking forward to seeing you again," he offered in a last ditch attempt to change her mind.

"I'd love to see her, but only, I repeat, only, in the limits of safe, comfortable Kansas City."

"Come on, Andy. You had a great time in the canyon, didn't you?" She stared at him until he shifted restlessly in his chair. "Well, didn't you?"

"I got sunburned, sprained, prickled, and peeled," she pointed out, enumerating each item on her fingertips. "The only time I wasn't terrified, I was mentally confused due to lack of liquids. It was, of course, the greatest time of my life. Do me a favor, Rick, and close the door on your way out."

She began riffling through papers on her desk. He rose, then dropped some pamphlets under her nose. "Have it your way," he said cheerily, "but I'll just leave you these brochures on Keystone and Arapaho in case you want to consider changing your mind."

"Out, Paisley," she ordered without looking up.

When the door snapped shut, she released her rigid control and dropped her head into her hands. Damn! How long would she continue to be tormented by memories, images, desires? How many more times would she hear Tif's voice, see his smile, and ache to feel his touch? Six weeks and she still trembled at the merest mention of anything remotely connected to that trip.

The first week after her return had been, unexpectedly, the easiest. Wrung out physically and emotionally, she hadn't had the energy to indulge in full-blown remorse. Catching up on her caseload had helped, too. But day by day, depression had crept in on her. She began to think of all the things she could have said, could have done, should not have said, should not have done. All the little things that might have made him want to see her again.

One night she'd found herself at the library checking out an armload of books on the Grand Canyon. Back at her Plaza apartment she'd gone through them like a starving man through a refrigerator. She gazed at the falls of Elves' Chasm captured in a half page of color and relived the enchanted day they'd spent there. Her fingertips traced the flat image of the crystal waterfall as if she could perhaps again feel the wonder of the misty spray. A raft thrust sideways in the churning foam of Lava Falls made her heart stop for several seconds. The redwall limestone of Marble Canyon, the forbidding schist walls of Granite Gorge, the bright blossoms of a prickly pear cactus. Each photo held a painful memory that was yet so bright she could not stop turning the pages.

The startling contrast of lightning flashing across a pink-hued sky caught and held her attention. For a time she dreamed, half-smiling, of the night she knocked the tent down upon them. Suddenly a vision of Tif sheltering in a tent with another woman dispelled her smile. Tif rubbing sunburn lotion on one faceless female, swimming in Tapeats Creek with another. Tif with an unknown woman on the next river trip and the next. Tif, head oarsman of the "love boats."

The books were slammed shut and returned the next day.

When September came and she knew Tif must be back in town, Andy threw herself into her work, taking on extra cases, pushing her endurance to the limit with the cases she had. Anything, exhaustion, burnout, anything was better than reminding herself what she no longer had, would never have.

By and large the exercise had helped. The mental discipline she applied to her court appearances aided her in blocking out her unhappiness. It was only at moments when she was forced to face her feelings that Andra acknowledged the depth of her pain. Like the day Rick had heaped packages of photos on her desk.

"You keep saying you'll make time to go through these, but I just checked the docket—with your schedule you won't have time until the turn of the century. So I'm making time for you."

She'd gone through them experiencing the same half-magical, half-miserable emotions she'd felt on the trip. She was tempted to keep one picture of Tif squatting by the grill, steaming mug in hand and sleepy smile curving his lips, but she was afraid Rick would notice it missing, afraid of what it would reveal.

Then there was Rick's latest scheme. He was crazy; she

was sure of it. She wouldn't go to the corner with him, much less to a condominium in Colorado for a week. Not even to see Karla again. Being with them, seeing their happiness together, would only emphasize her own emotional deprivation while stirring up all the memories again and again.

On her way out that night she stopped by Rick's office and lay the brochures on the middle of his desk. She didn't really expect him to get the hint. Rick was the sort of guy who had to be hit with a brick to understand the building was falling down. But this time no impulse was going to overcome her determination to refuse him.

He cornered her two days later as she left Judge Hanson's chambers. "I've found us a fourth to share the condo," he said without preamble as he swung his briefcase to his left hand and grabbed her arm with his right.

She rolled her eyes. "Don't you ever give up?"

"No. Why do you think I'm such a terrific attorney?"

"I didn't think you were such—"

"Let's not get insulting," he cut in as he steered her out of the traffic in the hallway of the municipal court. "I'm not asking you to make a definite decision now—"

"Too bad. I have. I'm not going."

"—But just to meet this guy."

Andy stopped at that, pivoting to look at Rick. The seams of his suit threatened to rip across his brawny frame; the knot of his thin striped tie appeared ready to choke him. But it was the innocence on his bulldog face that disturbed Andy. "Guy?"

"Hey, it's not what you think. In fact, he'd like to meet you for lunch to see if you two would get along." He dashed toward the closing double doors of courtroom number 3, pausing to call over his shoulder, "I told him to pick you up at your office at one."

As she stamped back to the law firm, she visualized herself as a cartoon character with steam coming out of her ears. She'd meet this stranger, explain that Rick was thoroughly mistaken, and send him on his way. Though she had no intention of lunching with Rick's friend, she nonetheless stopped by the ladies' room to sweep a brush through her orderly curls and touch up her makeup. Vanity, she reprimanded herself before straightening the set of her fawn wool dirndl skirt and pleated cream blouse.

She was restlessly shuffling files from one edge of her desk to another, waiting for the receptionist to call her with word that her guest had arrived, when a soft rap preceded the opening of her door. Looking up, Andra's fixed smile congealed.

More tanned, more sun-bleached than ever, Tif stepped into her office, filling it to capacity. He shut the door, then paused, looking unaccustomedly uncertain. "Hello, Andy."

It had been nearly three years since she'd seen him in a suit. She'd forgotten how striking, how impressive, he looked fully dressed. The smoke-gray of his suit deepened the gray of his eyes while giving emphasis to the tawny hue of his skin, the silvered blond of his hair. He was so brilliantly handsome, so tall, so . . . so *everything!*

Andra realized her mouth hung open and shut it. "What are you doing here?" she demanded. She wasn't prepared for this!

"I've come to see you, to talk to you."

"You'll have to leave. I'm expecting someone." Her voice was brittle. Something flashed in his gray eyes. Her own brown eyes widened. "You're Rick's friend."

It had been a flat statement of certain fact, but Tif responded as if answering a question. "Yes. I . . . wasn't sure you'd want to see me again. If I'd called, would you have agreed to go out with me?"

She avoided his gaze. "Yes, of course. It's good to see old . . . friends."

A thick, oppressive silence descended. Andy fiddled

with the coil of her phone cord and looked everywhere but at Tif. He stood with the motionless poise only he was capable of, staring, she knew, directly at her.

"How are you?" inquired Tif with the remote politeness of a chance-met stranger.

"Fine. I'm fine," she answered stiffly.

"Rick says you've been overworking."

Only to keep from tormenting myself with thoughts of you. "Not really," she said.

Another awkward silence draped itself over them. Andra shifted nervously. Why had he come? To talk, he said. She wanted to hope for more, yet dared not. She picked up her purse.

"Well," she said, her voice tinsel bright, "shall we go to lunch and talk over old times?"

"I don't want to talk over old times."

The intimate caress in his tone brought Andy's gaze flying up to his. Her throat closed. There was such a mixture of expression there—longing, hesitancy, caution, and something more, something Andy couldn't define. She cleared her throat.

"If you've come to talk me into going to Colorado, forget it. I never had any intention of going."

He took a step forward. She took one back.

"I think you'd like skiing. I'd like to be the one to teach you," he told her, all the while moving closer as she moved back.

In the tiny cramped space that was her office, Andy had nowhere else for retreat. She leaned against the bookcase behind her desk and stared up at him. "You would?"

Though he did not touch her, she could feel the warmth of his body. God, how she yearned to wrap herself in that warmth!

"Marry me, Andra."

Her heart stopped. She knew she couldn't have heard what she'd thought she'd heard. She shook her head, trying to unclog her ears. She parted her lips to ask him to repeat that, please, when he gently pressed two fingers against her mouth.

"I can understand your refusal," he said in a quick, short rasp. "But let me explain, let me at least apologize for my behavior this summer. If you . . . if then you still feel the same, I promise not to bother you again. But hear me out, Andy, before you throw away our future."

Stunned, she could only nod her head. Inside, her confused mind shouted, *Are you crazy? Of course I'll marry you!* He removed his fingertips, and she managed to croak through burning lips, "Tif—"

"Listen to me before you say anything, Andy." He wheeled and paced the short width of her office. "God knows I never meant to fall in love with you. The last thing I needed in my life was another woman wrapped up in her career. I knew . . . I thought I knew that being an attorney meant more to you than anything, *anyone* else. I couldn't go through that again."

"Oh, Tif, I—"

"Andy, please!" He faced her, his face tortured. "Maybe we should have gone for lunch first. I need a drink." Abruptly, he dropped onto the arm of a chair. Studying his knuckles, he continued in a flat tone, "Even when I began to realize you weren't capable of putting me through the sort of emotional wringer Carol did, I couldn't accept my feelings for you. I expected more rejection, more torment, and frankly, I didn't have the courage to put it to the test. Not even after I knew I loved you."

"When?" Her query wisped thinly. She scarcely dared breathe.

"The day at Elves' Chasm. I asked you to . . . love me. You thought I meant—well, hell, that's what I thought I was asking! Until I said it. Then I realized I wanted you to *love* me."

A mist of memories cascaded over them, holding them

in captivated silence. For a moment the idyllic beauty of travertine formations, graceful waterfalls, and a clear blue pool seemed to enfold them. Then Tif jerked to his feet, dispelling the mist.

Shoving his hands in his pockets, rumpling his gray suit, he muttered, "The closer we came to the end of the trip, the less I wanted to love you. I resented you for making me love you. When you demanded a commitment for the future, I felt as if I'd been kicked in the stomach. I couldn't see how we could possibly make it, juggling our careers with a home life. I'd been through that once, and I swore I'd never go through it again. So I reacted like an angry adolescent. I'm sorry."

She was certain he could hear the wild coursing of her blood in her veins, the fierce clamoring of her heart in her chest. She wondered how he could stand there, gazing at her with pain-darkened eyes, and not hear and feel and know how much she loved him.

She took a step, whispering, "Tif—"

Once again he cut her off, yanking his hands from his pockets and gesturing to halt her movement. "But after you'd gone, I realized what an ass I'd been. How many chances do we get at love? I'd thrown my chance away . . ."

His voice ached with the loss he felt. The bones of his face shifted, tightening in pain. He reached toward her. "I've spent the summer aching for you. Let me touch you, kiss you. Just once more."

If this were a dream, Andy didn't want to wake up. Wraithlike, she floated into his outstretched arms. She strained against him, wanting the reassurance of reality. She felt the taut musculature of him beneath the slickness of his suit.

"You feel . . . different . . . like this," she sighed.

"Like how?"

"Dressed."

His hands stilled, resting on the roundness of her hips. "Oh, god, Andy, you tempt me . . ." he moaned into her ear. She wiggled and he tightened his hold on her.

"If you'd only let me speak, I'd have accepted your proposal ten minutes ago," she confessed on a breathy laugh.

Tif drew back, disbelief and desire warring in his eyes. "But you shook your head—"

"I couldn't believe my ears. In fact, I'm wondering if this isn't a dream."

The constrictive squeeze of his arms about her proved this was no dream. He nuzzled his lips against her neck and murmured a litany of love words. She was his darling, his sweet, his love. He curled his palm over the fullness of her breast, forever ruining the crisp pleats of her blouse. He sought the softness of her buttocks through the layers of her wool skirt. Flicking his tongue over the shell of her ear, he said between ragged breaths, "A dozen times I had phone in hand to call you. But I was sure you'd tell me to get lost, hang up, refuse to listen . . ."

She hushed him with lips that promised never to refuse him. All the doubt and hesitation fled before the passionate certainty of that kiss.

As if they might somehow meld together into one being, they pressed closer, closer, until the curves of one ground into the hollows of the other. Soaring with passion, swaying with pleasure, they stumbled, then overbalanced, breaking apart. Tif quickly righted and held onto Andy. They wobbled unsteadily, then laughed.

Suddenly, Tif scooped her up and lifted her to the edge of her desk. He stood, legs apart, arms braced against the wood, straddling her. "How's the ankle?"

"Okay now. You were right; it was a severe sprain. The doctor wanted me to use crutches, but I limped about instead for several weeks. It's back to normal now, though, see?" She raised her leg, exhibiting the mobility of her slim hosed ankle.

"Prettiest ankle I've ever seen," he said, catching hold of it. He stooped and kissed the turn of her ankle. Slowly sliding his hand over the curve of her calf, he inspected her leg as if it were the first he'd ever seen.

Shivering with excitement, Andy half-gasped, half-laughed. Tif raised his darkened eyes to hers while his fingers continued their mesmerizing climb upward. She licked her lips, and his lashes flickered. He leaned forward to kiss her.

"I kept your T-shirt," she blurted absurdly.

"Ummm, I know," he said, concentrating on exploring her throat with his lips.

Her pulse catapulted as he nibbled the flesh above the collar of her blouse. "To sleep in," she mumbled in confusion.

He stopped nibbling, and she moaned weakly in protest. "You sleep in my T-shirt?" he asked in tones of wonderment.

Speech was beyond her. She nodded.

"I love you," he groaned. "From the top curl"— he kissed this—"to the bottom toe. Every square inch. I love you."

She lay her hands over his, fastening them to her breasts. "Tif . . . I . . . this summer . . ." She hesitated, then went on in a rush, "I've spent countless hours imagining you traveling down the Colorado with other women." She lowered her lashes to hide her pain, but her voice trembled with accusation.

He set his lips briefly on her hands. Drawing back, he shook his head. "Why do you persist in believing me to be some sort of swinging ladies' man? Even if I were the type, what makes you think I exude that kind of appeal?"

"This . . ." she rasped, brushing her fingers over his eyelids. "And this . . ." She caressed the squared tilt of his lips. "And this . . ." She skimmed her fingers over his chest, floating further downward. "And most of all . . ."

He groaned and passionately pulled her to him. "Darling, there were no others. I was so damn pure the guys started calling me the monk. I told you, I'm strictly a one-woman man."

Doubt stabbed at Andy's happiness, piercing it. A one-woman man. He was that, all right. But was Carol still that woman? Was she the substitute for the woman he couldn't have?

She gnawed on her lower lip. A frown came into Tif's eyes as he followed the motion. He tapped her lip. "Don't do that. You shouldn't bite on my property that way."

"Your property?"

"We're getting married; those lips are mine," he told her firmly. "The same goes for the rest of this luscious body of yours. You've got to start taking more care of it, for my sake."

His playful teasing didn't chase away her remembered fears. The specter of Carol hung over her. Folding her hands together in her lap, she stared straight at his navy silk tie and confronted this ghost. "What about Carol?" she asked in a voice void of expression.

"Carol?"

She glanced up, saw his evident puzzlement, and looked away. "I know how much you still love her. I've seen signs of it over and over again. I . . . can live with that, I guess, but I . . . need to know if I'm just a . . . a substitute . . ."

Her words trailed away into an ominous silence. She couldn't look at him. She was afraid of the truth she'd see in his eyes. He still loved Carol; it was true. She felt her newfound happiness shatter into a thousand splinters at her feet.

"Did I say once that you were incredibly dumb?" he finally asked. "That was a massive understatement."

Her head whipped up; her eyes searched his. "Don't you?"

"If you mean, don't I love Carol, the answer is no. Irrevocably, unalterably no. I loved her once, long ago, resented her for years, even hated her at times, and still feel a mixture of emotions too tangled for description whenever I think of her. But I do not, definitely and finally, do not love her."

Tif leaned his muscled form into her soft curves. "I love you, Andra. You and only you. I want to marry you and work to make a lifetime together. If that means playing second banana to a courtroom and a jury, well, I'll learn to accept that. I'll have to. I need you."

Unbidden tears trickled down Andra's cheeks. She tried to speak, couldn't, and ended by burying her head in his shoulder. His arms enveloped her protectively. This was love such as she'd never dared hoped to find.

After a bit she raised her head, snuffling. A handkerchief fluttered before her nose, and she took it from his hand thankfully. She blew her nose and smiled feebly. "I'm sorry. It's just so much, so unexpectedly. If you knew how long I've loved you . . ."

"I look forward to hearing in great detail."

"I think I was attracted to you way back then. At the divorce," sniffed Andy. She peeped over the white linen to see him gazing at her with an arrested expression on his face.

"Were you? I wish I'd known," he began, then stopped. He lightly, reverently, kissed the top of her dark hair. "No, on second thought, it wouldn't have been the same then. I was too embittered to love you then."

"As long as you love me now, nothing else matters," she said fiercely. "Nothing means as much to me as you do.

I could never put my career before you, darling Tif, not ever. You mean too much to me."

He engulfed her tightly in his arms, nearly strangling her in his clasp. "We'll work it out, honey! Your career, mine, the rafting, everything!"

"The rafting?" she echoed faintly.

"Well, I rather thought we might team during the summers." Pulling away slightly, he dazzled her with a sparkling grin.

"Oh, I don't see how," she protested with a determined shake of her head. "My schedule would never—"

"We'll do what we can," he countered.

"But, I was such a rotten rafter." She gestured broadly, flourishing her hands for emphasis.

"You were terrific. A little on the clumsy side, maybe, but you'll get better." He caught hold of her waving hands, stilling them. "I even thought that maybe in a few years we could run our own commercial float operation, work together year round."

"Oh, my god," moaned Andra as her life flashed before her eyes.

"Think of the advantages. We'd be together all the time."

"You're mad, you know that? It would never work. For one thing—"

"I realize that no one can raise objections like an attorney," cut in Tif, kissing her hands, "but in this case, my dear, let your husband—almost—be the judge."

"But—" she began.

"Objection overruled."

"Bu—mumph—"

"Overruled," he repeated firmly, muffling her lips with his.

LOOK FOR NEXT MONTH'S
CANDLELIGHT ECSTASY ROMANCES ®

154 A SEASON FOR LOVE, *Heather Graham*
155 LOVING ADVERSARIES, *Alana Smith*
156 KISS THE TEARS AWAY, *Anna Hudson*
157 WILDFIRE, *Cathie Linz*
158 DESIRE AND CONQUER, *Diane Dunaway*
159 A FLIGHT OF SPLENDOR, *Joellyn Carroll*
160 FOOL'S PARADISE, *Linda Vail*
161 A DANGEROUS HAVEN, *Shirley Hart*